The Seasons

A native of Georgia, USA, **SONJA LEWIS** moved in the late 90s to London, where she lives with her husband, Paul. Her first collection of short stories, *The Seasons* draws from both American and British culture, taking rich snapshots of poignant moments in the lives of some extraordinary characters. Author of *The Barrenness* and *The Blindsided Prophet*, Sonja writes a *Huffington Post* UK blog, also.

The Seasons

A Collection of Short Stories

SONJA LEWIS

Prymus Publications
London

The Seasons
A Prymus Publication/2014
Published simultaneously in Great Britain and the United States

All rights are reserved
©2014, Sonja Lewis

ISBN – 978-0-9567105-6-7 (trade paperback)

Book Design by www.KarrieRoss.com
Cover images istockphoto.com

For Lendon Lewis
&
For Dalia Warner
'For whom winter came all too early'

For my aunt, Dorothy L. Hubbard,
who left in early winter but will
abide in my heart and mind
throughout all seasons.

CONTENTS

Spring

"Youth is like spring,
an over-praised season more
remarkable for biting winds
than genial breezes."

~Samuel Butler

Scout Gets Her Tongue Back

SCOUT HASN'T TALKED IN FIVE YEARS. Though she makes sounds that get her grandmother's attention. Teddy holds her gently and smooths her hair. She whispers softly into her ear.

"It's all right, baby. It's all right," she says. "Shush now. Teddy's here."

Scout wriggles out of her arms and stares into her worn eyes. Teddy looks like her mom, pretty but like a Raggedy Ann doll. She dresses like Raggedy Ann, too, her clothes blousy and colourful—yet dingy. Her hair is long and stringy. Now it's covered with a vibrant scarf, and she wears a flowered nightgown.

Scout longs to tell Teddy about the bad dream that woke her—her dad carrying her mom through the living room, her with limp, dangling arms and eyes popped wide open. She feels the tears streaming down her face. She opens her mouth, searches for the voice deep within herself. She can almost feel it at the pit of her stomach, but she can't force it to move up to her throat and come out of her mouth, even if she moves her lips.

Scout curls up on the pillow. "It's all right, baby," Teddy says again, caressing her. "It will come. Try to go back to sleep." She feels her grandma's warm presence and can hear her breathing. She closes her eyes.

Scout remembers the day she last talked, which is also the day she last saw her parents. But she isn't sure whether her last words were spoken or just thought.

"Nothing, Daddy," she had said or thought. "Nothing. Just Mommy in your arms."

Like in the dream, she had seen her dad carrying her mom, but her mom was awake, her big eyes shiny like quarters. Also, Scout thought for sure she had been smiling. It was nice to see them acting like Mommy and Daddy again. A little earlier they had been fussing and fighting terribly.

That morning, shortly after the doorbell rang, Scout heard her mother shouting.

"I am still young, damn it," she said. "I should have never married your old ass." Her cursing made Scout's chest pound. It would only make her father angrier. He didn't like swearing.

"Watch your filthy mouth," he said. "You are going to find yourself without her if you keep this up."

"I'm sick of your threats!" she screamed. "Who are you to threaten me? She's my baby, too. I had her—or have you forgotten?"

Scout's stomach tightened as they neared her room. She had rushed from the bathroom only moments ago and struggled into the ugly dress her mom said she had to wear, even if she didn't like it.

"No," Scout had said. "I want to wear my jeans."

Alternate Saturdays she slouched, played basketball, watched television. But this was not an alternate Saturday. It was her time to be with her father and wear ugly dresses made of silk and satin with big bows and sashes.

"Get up, Scout!" her mom had said.

"Why do I have to do what he says?" Scout asked, noticing that her mom was wearing a short black sundress and high heels. "You don't."

Her mom gripped her face and stared at her with big, round eyes. "Your father is not my father, he is yours. Now stop sassing me and get up!"

Scout had allowed herself to be marched to the bathroom, but now she was back in her room, dreading their entrance.

Her father looked like the tall and skinny man in the circus, performing an act. He wore a long, white coat and a stethoscope around his neck. He shot her a fake smile and stopped short of her. He noticed the yellow M&Ms wrapper on the dresser.

"What is all this?" He tossed the wrapper in the air. It floated to the floor, making Scout dizzy. "What is it?"

Scout kept quiet, watching her mom open and close drawers and shove clothes into her bag. She had already scolded Scout about eating the candy in the middle of the night. Sometimes she acted like she didn't notice when Scout ate junk, but when her dad was coming around, she got mad. He was a doctor. He didn't like junk food.

"Somebody answer me!" her father shouted.

Though her mom had tidied the rest of the room earlier, hiding her softball and baseball bat in her toy chest, Scout's basketball was in the middle of the floor, and her blue blanket with imprints of basketballs lay across the arm of her rocking chair. Still ignoring her father, her mom picked up the blanket and crammed it into the bag.

Her dad pulled it out and flung it across the room. "She's not a boy, Zelda," he snapped. "Anyhow, she's too big for a blanket."

"You tell her that," her mother said, reaching for the blanket.

"Okay, I will," he said and looked at Scout. Then he grabbed her mother by her thin arm and yanked her close to him.

Her mother's eyes widened. She tried to pull herself away, but he dragged her closer.

"You been smoking around her," he said. Scout lowered her gaze. She had smelled her mom's cigarette breath this morning when she hugged her.

"Why do you smoke?" Scout had asked then. "Daddy says cigarettes are bad for you."

"He's right," she said. "Sometimes Mommy gets it wrong, but you don't have to follow. Do as Daddy tells you. Remember, he is your father, not mine!"

Now their voices jerked Scout out of her thoughts and brought her back into the hot room.

"I have told you for the last time that your behaviour is unacceptable. I've got a good mind not to bring her back here."

"You can't do that!" her mom yelled.

Scout tripped over her basketball and slipped on the floor. Although she did not feel any pain, she felt embarrassed, so she cried. Her dad picked her up, and her mom pulled at her. They tussled over her, making her cry even more.

Her dad pushed her mom away and hauled Scout to his Jeep. Her mom trailed them, hitting him with her fists. Mrs. Maple, the neighbor, was standing at the fence, her eyes fixed on them. Her two long plaits hung to her shoulders.

Mrs. Maple turned away and went back inside. But her cat pulled at Scout's dad's pants leg and stared at him with green fierce eyes. He stomped, and the cat scrambled. Hurriedly, her dad put her in the car and told her to stay. Her mom huffed off and rushed back into the house. Her dad ran after her, and from what Scout could tell he pushed his way in.

The car was nice and cool. She listened to the humming engine, feeling her heart settle down.

Scout had witnessed such fights before, but this one seemed to go on forever. She waited and waited. She tried to think of something other than her mom and dad. But she couldn't, so she got out and tiptoed back to the front door. That's when she saw him carrying her mother across the living room towards the bedroom, but it wasn't like the nightmare. Her mom seemed lively.

Her face plastered to the screen door, Scout waited. She felt hot, like a doll melting. Then her father came rushing into the hallway but stopped abruptly when he saw Scout and dropped a plastic bucket.

Her dad's eyes were wild, like the wolves she had seen on television. He hurried toward her and burst through the door, yelling, "How long have you been here, Scout?"

She fished for an answer, but her voice was stuck in her stomach. He grabbed her and shook her until she cried.

"What did you see?" he demanded.

That's when she said—or thought she said—she saw him carrying her mom.

"Never speak of this again," he said, now squeezing her arms. "Never!"

She was about to tell him he was hurting her, but somehow he sensed it. His look softened. With sweaty hands, he pulled her close to him, squeezed her until he hurt her even more. He whispered over and over again, "Daddy never meant to hurt you."

Scout felt what was left of her voice at the pit of her stomach. Her dad picked her up and rushed her to the car.

Scout didn't remember much about the drive, except that it was eerily quiet and the air smelled of gasoline. Her stomach hurt most of the time. Her father gave her more medicine, maybe Pepto-Bismol, like her mom had given her that morning when she said her stomach hurt from eating the M&Ms. It soothed her and made her sleep.

She woke up when they stopped once or maybe twice to eat or to use the bathroom. He took her to McDonald's for food and into the boys' bathroom. Neither of them spoke.

In the car, he drove fast and listened to the radio. He flipped the dial repeatedly. And he talked on his cellular phone in a language that Scout did not understand.

They drove for a long time. When they got to where they were going, her grandpa's house, which they normally flew to, she saw police cars everywhere. Her grandfather—a doctor, too—came outside and stared at them through watery eyes. In his blue jean overalls, he looked older than Scout remembered.

Her grandfather told her father he was glad his mother wasn't alive to witness his downfall. Then he took Scout by the hand and led her into the house.

That day was the last time she saw either of her parents.

The next morning, Scout is glad it's Saturday. She doesn't have to go to that crazy school, where the children are unruly. Some can't walk; others can't talk very well, but they still tease her that the cat has got her tongue.

She hates her school and thinks about her old one all the time. She wishes she could go back there. She wishes her mom hadn't died.

Now, though, she goes outside to get the mail. Immediately, she notices a dead bird on the walkway. Ants crawl over its flesh. It looks as if someone has skinned it, perhaps only this morning. It lies on its side, a wing broken.

Scout pulls the skirt of her denim dress between her legs. Stoops to get a closer view and whiffs the bird's smell. It smells fresh, like the air on a hot day. She wonders if her mom smelled like this after she died instead of cigarette smoke mixed with sweet perfume.

She stands and steps back. Her head spins, remembering her mom when she tickled her, hugged her, and sometimes fell on the bed and read to her. She never saw her dead, but Teddy says she is definitely dead. She was cremated.

Teddy often cries, big thick tears, when she talks about her only daughter. Scout looks at her and cries, too.

Now she jumps at Teddy's voice. "You're supposed to get the mail, honey," her grandmother says. "Come on in now. I've got breakfast ready!"

Scout tries to move her legs—the mailbox is only a few feet away—but she studies the bird still, wondering what happened to it. Did another bird harm it? Did a squirrel sneak up on it and steal its skin?

She can't help thinking the bird and her mother are one and the same. One day they were both flitting around, and the next gone. She thinks of her dad, too. The police took him away. After her grandfather took her inside that day, Scout peeked out the window and saw the police take her father off in handcuffs. Later a police officer and a lady came to see her grandfather. They questioned him and threatened to take Scout away. But he convinced them to let her stay, leave her alone. She was only five.

Teddy came the next day and took Scout home with her. She said she had to fight to keep her. That's what she told her friend on the telephone. But she won. Scout wondered what she meant, but she couldn't talk, so she couldn't ask.

Teddy calls her name again, wrenching her out of her daydream. Gnats swarm around her head. Her face is wet with tears.

Teddy comes toward her, wearing a flowing sundress. She carries a shovel. Her sunglasses cover her eyes. Her brown skin glistens. Far away, she could be Zelda, Scout's mother. She has curves like a mother, not a grandmother.

All the kids at school say she is Scout's mother. And sometimes she acts like her mom. She guesses Scout's needs all the time. She knows when Scout wants to eat, to sleep, to be alone. She knows. And she knows what kind of clothes Scout likes—T-shirts, jeans, and denim dresses—not frilly dresses like her dad wanted her to wear.

She reads to her from *Mary Poppins* and *Charlotte's Web*. Then she leaves the books with her. She knows that Scout has nightmares, so Teddy lets her sleep in her bed, and she comforts her. Now she somehow knows that Scout wants to bury the dead bird.

Teddy hands Scout the shovel, the handle long and slender. Scout moves the bird with the tip of the shovel, revealing the wet space under its body. A speck of blood is there. She feels an urge to touch it, but she doesn't. She lifts the bird on the shovel. It's really light. The ants retreat to a crevice in the pavement.

Her arms feel weak as she notices how still the bird is. Suddenly, it dawns on her that when her father carried her mother across the living room floor, she was still, too. Scout sees the scene in her mind's eye again, only this time it is very much like the nightmare.

She will make sure the bird gets a proper burial.

In the backyard, she lays the bird to the side while she digs a hole. Two birds stand at the edge of the lawn watching. They stay still, then flap their wings.

Teddy drops to her knees in her pretty dress and begins digging the red clay with her fingers. She totally loses herself in the activity, like one of the kids at school coloring a picture. She crumbles the dirt in her hands and smells it. When the hole is deep enough, Scout tips the bird in. The two live birds make tweeting noises and peck at the grass in the distance.

Again Scout thinks of the last day she saw her mother. The house burned; Teddy said it did—Scout heard her say it on the telephone. She remembers how the car smelled of gasoline and the big bucket her father had been carrying.

These thoughts make her stomach hurt.

The bird's eye that she can see is still wide open. Scout dumps dirt, red and rich, over the bird, covering its eye first. Her mother's eyes were wide open, too. Teddy puts some dirt on, as well, and then pats the grave with her slender hands. She rocks on her knees.

One of the birds pecks near Scout's foot. Scout notices the bird looking at her; it has round brown eyes. It wants to know what she is thinking. Does she know what happened to the other bird? When she doesn't say anything, the bird pecks her toe. Its bill is short and pointed and stings like a needle prick.

Ouch, she thinks and maybe says. She is not sure whether the word comes out or not. But her grandmother makes a sound and pulls off her sunglasses and stares at her. Teddy's eyes are fiery red.

Now Scout feels the heat of the sun breathing on her back. The lump in her stomach rises to her throat. Tears pour from her grandmother's eyes, dripping everywhere. Scout wonders why she is crying. Maybe she cries for no reason, too. The bird pecks her again. Suddenly, the lump slips away as if it were a plug that has been lodged in her throat. Her voice rises up in her, shoots through her body, and comes out.

"Ouch!" she says, the word slipping out loud and clear.

Teddy screams joyfully. The bird moves away. Still on her knees, her grandmother crawls to her, embraces her, and squeezes her tight.

"Baby, you spoke!" she says. "Thank you, God. Thank God!"

Scout feels like she is choking, but she somehow knows Teddy needs to cling to her. She hears the flapping of wings. She looks up and sees the two birds flying away. All of a sudden, they are airborne, joining a group of birds. They soar, looking pretty, very pretty.

"Look," she wriggles away from her grandmother and points at them.

Teddy looks up at the sky, too. Scout wonders where the birds are going. She remembers a song from Sunday school about flying away someday. Out of the blue, she wonders if her mother has flown away.

Though she feels a bit tongue tied, she knows she has her tongue back, so she stares hard at Teddy and asks, "Do people fly away after they die?"

Her grandmother hugs her tightly again and then looks at her.

"Yes," she says. "They have to get to Heaven somehow, don't they?"

Scout thinks of her mom in Heaven, flying around with the birds, the angels. She smiles shyly at Teddy.

Her grandmother pulls up from the ground and takes her hand. Suddenly, Scout feels hungry, and like she has a lot to say. Slowly, she and Teddy walk into the house together.

Reggie
Grows Up

ODESSA WAKES ME UP WITH DAYLIGHT this morning and tells me to dress in a yellow shirt and khaki pants. Normally, I sleep late on Saturday, and so does she. But today, she acts like it is Sunday, the day we go to church.

"We can't be late, Reggie," my mom says quietly and turns to the big red suitcase she has laid out.

Yesterday she stayed home from her summer teaching job and washed and pushed the iron over my shirts and pants until all the wrinkles dropped out. Then she hung the clothes in the closet.

Now she is putting my clothes in the suitcase.

"Where are we going," I ask. Odessa doesn't answer and keeps packing.

I have only needed a suitcase twice. The first was when we moved from Granny's house to here with my stepfather, Johnny. Here we have lots of trees. I like them as long as they are not next to my window, throwing shadows.

I hope we are not moving again, certainly not away from my job, right up the road from our house. I go to the Work Place everyday on a small bus. There I sit on the back porch and shell peas and plop them into a big dishpan. But that's when it's hot. When it cools down, I pick up pecans and throw them into a big burlap sack. When it gets full, my boss throws it across his shoulder and hurls it onto the back of a truck. Then, when it gets so cold that I can see my breath, I work inside. I sometimes hand my boss things, the right nails or sacks, or I sweep up the sawdust. That takes me a long time.

And everyday when I leave work, I go to Granny's until Odessa picks me up. At Granny's I call my girlfriend, April, and play with my Game Boy until *Jerry Springer* comes on. And when Odessa takes me home, I go straight to my room. I even eat there if she lets me. Then she calls me into the bathroom and helps me bathe. But for a long time now, Johnny has been helping me because I'm twenty-seven, a man, now. Still, Odessa doesn't treat me like a man. Johnny doesn't, either. They won't let me marry April, even though my cousin, Raven, who's twenty-seven, married her boyfriend and had Tiara with him.

Last week, I packed myself to move in with April. Earlier that day I proposed to her in the cafeteria at work after seeing Fat Joe holding her hand. At first, I watched for a minute, noticing that April was wearing the same red dress with a black bow that she was wearing when we became boyfriend and girlfriend. Then I ran up to them and tried to pry Joe's hand away from April's, but he held tight and pushed me to the floor.

"What is April to you?" Joe asked, snarling.

"She, she my girlfriend," I said, noticing that other boys and girls had gathered around. With big, light brown eyes, April looked down at me. But she didn't say anything.

"What makes you think she's your girlfriend?" Joe asked.

"I eat lunch with her everyday, call her everyday when I get home, and dream about her. She's my girlfriend."

"That don't mean nothing," he said, looking from me to April. She batted her eyelids. "Nothing!"

"That's not true," I said. "She's been my girlfriend for five months. We got together on my birthday in February. Didn't we, April?"

She nodded.

"Well, I don't care how long she been your girlfriend," he said. "You don't have no papers on her. She ain't your wife, so you can't tell me not to hold her hand."

That's when I asked April to marry me. I asked three times.

She smiled, showing her deep dimples and pretty white teeth, and said yes. Then she squinted and tossed her long brown hair. "Where is my ring?" she asked.

"I'll bring it tomorrow," I said.

April smiled widely and clapped her hands together.

"You ain't got no money," Joe said, standing over me. "How are you going to buy a ring?"

"I already got it," I said, remembering the ring my daddy gave Odessa.

I spat at him. He kicked me, and I kicked him back as much as I could. Then he pounced on me and started choking me. I thought I was going to smother and was glad when my boss stopped him. Still, we both got put out of work for two days for fighting.

When I stop thinking about this, I notice Odessa still packing.

"Is April coming with us?" I ask.

"Don't mention April to me, Reggie," Odessa says. "She's the reason we're in this mess now."

I drop my head, going back to my thoughts. I remember that Odessa doesn't like April. She doesn't want me to marry her. And it is her fault that I didn't move in with April.

The same day I proposed to April, I tried to go to her house after we got home, but because I walk slowly with a limp, Odessa caught me before I got out of the driveway and made me come back inside. I told her how much I love April and about how I feel funny when I talk to her and think about her. I want to kiss her , tell her I love her, but every time I try, I get scared.

Odessa told me to shut up.

"You shut up," I said. "I, I grown."

"You're not!" she yelled. "You're more stupid than I thought!"

My heart thumped so loud, I thought it would pop. And she kept right on fussing. "I'm not going to put up with this, Reginald," she said. "Every time you can't have what you want, you do something crazy. When you were younger, you went crazy over Raven, your own cousin, remember? Then you hit the minivan driver one day because he wouldn't let you go home with April. You have to stop this nonsense."

"I'm going to marry April!" I yelled. I held up the ring I'd taken from Odessa's jewelry box.

"What?" she screamed. "You've stolen my ring. Give it to me now!"

"My daddy bought it. You said I could have it one day." She reached for it, but I held it tightly. "No! Leave me alone. I grown. It's mine."

Odessa's face turned dark. She grabbed my hand and pried the ring out of it. That's when I spat in her face. She threw her hands over her mouth. So then I punched her in the forehead.

Suddenly, she grabbed me by the collar and shook me until I felt dizzy. I managed to get myself away from her and swat at her again, but she caught my hands and held them together. When I felt my wrists aching, she let go and backed away from me.

"That's it, Reggie," she said, breathing loudly. "You have written your own ticket. You want to be grown. Then be grown. I cannot do this anymore."

Then she rushed out of the room and pulled the door closed. I tried to get out, but I couldn't open the door until Johnny came home. By the time he reached me, my head was hurting, and my mouth felt like cotton was stuffed in it.

Johnny told me I could not hit my mother. He said this over and over again. I told him all I wanted was for Odessa to listen and on *Jerry Springer*, the people listen, at least for a little while, if someone makes them.

My stepfather patted me on the back and dropped his head. The next day, he took me to the doctor, a short white man, who said he would give me something to help control my hormones. I didn't know what that meant, but it was the same thing he said last time and the time before. The shot stung at first, and then it made me woozy and tired for hours.

When I stop thinking about all this, I notice Odessa folding a shirt neatly and laying it on top of the other clothes. The suitcase looks full. Although I don't mention April anymore, I do ask again where we are going. Still, Odessa acts like she doesn't hear me and closes the suitcase and her eyes.

"Where are we going?" I ask again.

"Don't ask me that again, Reggie," she says, opening her eyes. I notice tears dripping down her jaws. "I have already told you."

I limp over to her. "Don't, don't cry, Odessa," I pat her on the back. She moves away from me and rushes out of the room.

Soon after she leaves the room, I sit in my special chair and play with my Game Boy. The sunlight comes through my curtains like a yellow ribbon. I like the way it feels on my face. Johnny comes in and leans against the door. He looks at me for a long time, and then he clears his throat. He asks me if I want to take my television and my PlayStation now or get them later.

"Where, where are we going?" I ask as he unhooks the television and the PlayStation. "Are we going to church?"

"No, we are not going to church, son," he mumbles and carries the television out first and then returns for the PlayStation.

He tells me it's time to go. I ask him if Odessa is going with us. He looks down at his tennis shoes. They are blue and white but look like my black ones.

"Yeah," he says. "She's waiting for us in the car."

I hobble behind Johnny to the car, cradling my Game Boy.

We drive to the other side of town. I know this because we go over the long bridge that separates east from west. I take a break from my game and look down at the water. It looks green and ugly. Johnny says we have a drought and we need rain. That is why the river looks dirty.

Odessa looks out the window. She has not said one word to me, but she does say two to Johnny when he asks her to talk to me. *F——- off.* He sighs and keeps driving.

We stop in front of a red brick house with lots of trees hanging over the yard. I think this must be scary at night, trees lurking at the window.

"Are you getting out?" Johnny asks Odessa.

She doesn't say anything and lowers her head.

"Okay, champ," he says, looking over into the back seat. "It's just us."

"Bull," she says. "How can you say that?"He yanks the car door open, gets out, and slams it.

I want to say something to Odessa, but I don't think it's good timing, so I wait for Johnny to help me out. I will see her later, I'm sure.

Johnny carries the suitcase. I carry my Game Boy. I wonder why Odessa is not coming in, and I keep looking back at her. Her face is plastered to the window. I almost trip over the jagged cement on the walkway, and when I look around, I see a fat lady with fluffy hair and small glasses.

She smiles and asks me if I'm Reggie. I nod. Johnny tells her they need to get the walkway fixed. It could hurt someone like me. She says they don't have the funding.

"I'll pay for it," he says firmly and sets the suitcase beside the door.

"Oh," she says in surprise. Then, "Come on in."

First, she shows us a big kitchen. Something about it is different. One thing is that they don't have big knives and forks like Odessa does. The lady fiddles with the knobs on the stove, assuring Johnny they're safe.

"We have been dealing with people like Reggie for years," she says.

Next, we go to a spacious room where two boys are watching television and one is playing with a Game Boy. I hear the bleeps and blasts. I say I like this room.

"Reggie can come to the game room anytime he likes," the lady says. "I'll show you his room."

While we walk down a narrow hallway, Johnny asks questions.

"Men and women do mix," the lady says in a whisper. "Our sister house is where the women stay, but we do monitor any visits. The girls are on contra-ceptives, and we teach the men about sexuality, too."

Johnny says something I can't make out.

"It is not a mistake, Mr. Law. It's reality," the lady says. "These young people have the same needs as the rest of us."

"I, I go to work from here?" I ask.

"Yes," she says. "Yes!"

I am relieved to hear this and follow her and Johnny to a small room with a teeny bed.

"This is your room, Reggie," she says. "Your bed."

"Where is Johnny's? Odessa's?"

The lady looks at Johnny. The room looks very dark, even after she turns the light on. A tree is lurking outside of the window. Suddenly, I feel scared and my stomach hurts.

"I don't like this room," I tell Johnny. "There's no television."

"Yours is in the car," Johnny says.

"Televisions are not allowed in bedrooms," the lady says and turns to me. She pushes her glasses up. "You can watch television anytime you like in the game room, Reggie."

"I watch it in my room," I say.

"You have a new room now," she says. "You'll get used to it, honey. It's a good room. Your parents are lucky to get you in here."

My Game Boy slips out of my hand. The lady and Johnny both turn to me and hold on to me. I am sweating more than I ever have before. Then I throw up all over myself. The lady opens a drawer and gets a towel. Johnny takes it and cleans me up.

Odessa comes out of nowhere and stops short of me and breaks down crying. On her knees, now hugging me, she says it's all her fault, she should never have brought me to this place, I'm too young to go out on my own, I'll never make it.

"He will not be on his own, Mrs. Law," the lady says. "The first few days are always the hardest. Why don't you let him talk to some of the other boys? Ask them?"

"It's not right," Odessa says and tells the lady to leave her alone with her son. Johnny and the lady step aside, but they talk loudly. All Odessa does is sob.

"She has to let go," the lady says.

"That's easier said than done," Johnny says. "Reggie is her only child."

"I understand that, but she doesn't have the skills to deal with him anymore."

"Maybe he can come home every weekend?"

"No," the lady says. "No! You have to give him a chance."

"You are saying all or nothing?"

The lady does not answer.

"We'll take nothing, then," Johnny says and comes back and takes me by the arm. I am trembling so much that when Odessa lets go of me and pulls herself up, Johnny has to hold me up.

He gets me to lean against him and hook my arms around him somehow. We leave together, me leaning against him. Outside I like the cool breeze in the air, and the trees look friendlier, but I still don't really like them. The boy who had been playing with his Game Boy runs out and calls my name.

"Here, Reggie, you left this!" I turn and see him with my Game Boy. He is chubby with funny eyes and fingers that curl like mine.

He hands me my Game Boy. "See you later!" He moves off, much faster than I could.

I cradle the game device, thinking he is nice, but I don't want to see him later if it means coming here.

Johnny helps me into the car and buckles my seat belt. He turns around and goes back for my suitcase. Odessa stands near the car door, pokes her head in, and wonders out loud if we ought to go to the hospital.

I don't want a shot, I tell her. I want to go home and sleep like I always do on Saturday. Then I promise her that I will not hit her again. Not ever!

"I not grown yet," I say.

She nods and smiles, though her eyes are watery. She gets into the car, and Johnny puts the suitcase in, and then he gets in, too. We drive home.

Summer

*"Summer is only the unfulfilled
promise of spring, a charlatan
in the place of the warm balmy
nights I dream of in April.
It is a sad season of life
without growth ...
It has no day."*

~F. Scott Fitzgerald

The Coloured Girl

THAT MORNING WHEN THE UNEXPECTED phone call came, Isabella Chiltern was sitting in her favourite chenille chair, flanked by luxurious cushions, reading *The Book of Chameleons.*

Only when she heard Anthony talking rather loudly did she glance up and quickly tuck her clandestine reading behind a cushion. One moment she saw her husband's ageing image through her highly hung mirror—its hand-carved frame covered in gold leaf— the next he was sidling up to her, wedging the phone between their heads.

"Mother is on the phone, too," he said loudly.

Isabella sat up straight, pressed her skirt with both hands and braced herself for Aidan's news. But when she heard her son's gleeful greetings and chit-chat about the weather, she somehow knew that whatever the news, it couldn't be too dreadful.

"So, darling," she interrupted, to what do we owe to this lovely surprise? We rarely hear from you these days and never at weekends. Is there something wrong?"

"On the contrary," Aidan said. "I have some rather good news."

"Do tell," Anthony chimed in.

"At last, I have a new partner," Aidan said happily.

Isabella felt her heart pounding. His divorce had been scarcely a year ago. She could hardly stop her mind from racing ahead. What did he mean by *partner?*

"Partner?" Anthony said jokingly. "Please don't tell us that you're coming out of the closet after suffering twenty-five years in a bad marriage, old chap."

Aidan laughed curtly. "Absolutely not, Father," he said. "You needn't worry. It's more like I have come out of a fog."

"Who is she then?" his father asked.

"Slim Withers is her name," he said, sounding quite besotted. "She's the most gorgeous creature the good Lord has ever made. I can't wait for you both to meet her. How about lunch tomorrow?"

"Lunch?" Isabella said questioningly, remembering their long-standing Sunday lunch at Anthony's club, where he'd been a member for donkey's years. They couldn't possibly invite Aidan and a new girlfriend along to that. Heavens knows they'd suffered enough scandal there already. "What about…?"

"Half past one?" Anthony interrupted.

Isabella moved away from the phone, folded her arms and shot him a heated stare. Was he mad, inviting this new person to the club? She shook her head violently, and mouthed "absolutely not". At the very least they should check her out first. Anyway, they'd never be able to fit two more people in at such short notice. Never!

She whispered, "Tea? What about tea? I could throw something together at the Lawns."

Anthony lowered his eyes and kept talking. "Yes, we'd love to meet her. Shall I find a spot then?"

"I thought we'd tag along at the club," Aidan said.

"Fully booked," Isabella said, leaning in closer to the phone again.

"Very well then," Aidan said. "I'll get Kate to find a spot halfway between Bucks and London."

They both agreed.

"Oh yes," he said, before ringing off, "there is one more thing." Isabella questioned Anthony with her eyes. He shrugged his shoulders. "Slim is African-American. Toodle-oo!"

It was just as well that Aidan had put the phone down. Isabella's voice had stuck in her throat and her husband was knocked for six, too. He somehow fell onto her, squashing her. She pushed him and fully expected him to have his say, but he got up, brushed himself off and proceeded to leave.

"Aren't you going to say something?" Isabella called after him.

"What is there to say?" he replied over his shoulder, without even looking back.

Isabella grabbed one of the cushions and hurled it in his direction. It hit the floor far short of him without so much as a sound. Exasperated, she dug out her book, found her place and began reading again. But try as she might to focus on the eccentric narrator of her novel, all she could think about was her own life becoming quite colourful.

The sun darted behind the clouds, casting a dreadful shadow over yet another spring day. The Chilterns waited at an odd restaurant, no better than some sort of American roadside café.

The lime-green tablecloth flapped in a brisk wind. Isabella hung onto her paper serviette, the same horrible colour as the tablecloth. She wished the staff would close the door. After all, they were standing around in attire featuring green vests and dicky bows, hands behind their backs, like they had nothing to do.

"The boy chose this place himself you know." Her husband fumbled with his napkin.

"No, darling, that secretary of his did."

"Poor girl did the best she could, I'm sure."

"Kate is anything but a poor girl," Isabella said. "But in her defence, I will say that any suitable place would have been fully booked weeks ago."

"We could have taken them to the club, you know." Anthony eyed Isabella.

She forced the paper napkin to stay on her lap.

"I think we've had enough embarrassment at the club, don't you, darling? You made sure of that!"

Anthony cleared his throat, held up his glass and inspected it. "What the devil sort of name is *Slim* for a girl anyway?"

"Oh, so you finally want to talk about the girl!" Isabella said. *Anything but your own dirty laundry,* she thought.

"What is there to talk about?" he asked, looking her up and down. "I only mentioned her name."

"Very well, then!" she said. Anthony knew that they needed to discuss the issue of Slim's race, but insisted on avoiding it. When she had mentioned the matter the night before, he had eyed her suspiciously then as well, and gone on to chastise her.

"You act like you've never met a coloured person," he had said.

"Of course I have," Isabella said defensively. She had met coloured people in the shops and so on, but if the truth were known, she had not had an encounter with one. All her housekeepers had been Filipina. Anthony, on the other hand, had had many opportunities as a retired senior partner in one of the most prestigious law firms in the country to meet all sorts of people.

"Isabella," Anthony called out to her. She glanced at him. "You must put this colour thing out of your mind before the girl gets here. If you don't, Aidan will see right through you. Neither of us wants that, do we?"

"You're right," she said quietly. Isabella took a sip of her water, noticing that the restaurant was now crowded and teeming with laughter and chatter. Still she kept worrying about their son's choice of partner. "It's just that Aidan has already had one bad marriage."

"Who said anything about marriage?" Anthony said, furrowing his brow. "The boy hasn't lost his marbles. He's already lost half of his fortune to one woman. Surely, he'll want to hang on to the rest." He gazed assuredly at Isabella. "This girl is an intriguing, new friend, nothing more!"

"Partner," Isabella said, gazing at her husband. "That suggests something serious."

"On the contrary," her husband said, pulling on his jacket. He stretched his neck. "It's a modern-day term of endearment, that's all. Ah, they're here."

Isabella patted the delicate pearls around her neck. "Aren't you glad you chose that blazer?" she asked, eyeing him.

"Not in the least," Anthony retorted. "I still say the ochre one was more appropriate. The girl will think I'm an old stuffy egg, dressed for the regatta."

"Surely, she won't judge a book by its cover."

Anthony grunted and shot her an ironic glance, then jumped up from his chair to receive their guests.

At first glance Slim looked svelte, like a model, just as Isabella imagined her own daughter would have been had she honoured the pregnancy. She somehow knew it would have been a girl. Her heart felt heavy, remembering her youthful past. Quickly, she put the thoughts aside and focused on her approaching son and his partner.

Up close, the girl was petite and perfectly shaped, with untamed curly hair, several curls falling over her forehead. Unable to calm her clacking chest, Isabella could hardly rise. She jerked when Aidan leaned over to kiss her. He wore an open-collar white shirt, the buttons undone down to his stomach. And that was not the worst of it. He sported a flashy earring in his left ear. She couldn't help buttoning up his shirt.

So this was what went on in Aidan's private life. No wonder they scarcely heard from him. Their grandson Andrew had tried to warn her.

"Dad thinks he's David Bowie or someone these days."

"What on earth do you mean, dear?"

"Just wait till you see him."

Now she fully understood.

Aidan stopped her from meddling with his shirt and introduced the girl, who extended her hand, exhibiting a flashy diamond ring. Dazzled by it, Isabella only caught snippets of the chit-chat. The girl was from Florida. She was named after her father, a retired jazz musician, nicknamed Slim. Hypocritically, Anthony said he rather liked her unusual name.

Before long, the four of them were sitting around the table, having a drink together. Isabella could hardly keep her eyes off the girl. She had perfect white teeth and a chiselled face that came to life when she smiled. Isabella imagined her to be a beautiful sculpture, grinning when no one watched. She wore a V-neck bronze pullover dress, almost the colour of her skin, which hugged her as if it had been painted on.

And her grammar was impeccable, albeit she had an American drawl. Isabella longed to tell her how wonderful she looked and sounded, but she contained herself.

It was Anthony who pointed out that her skin was absolutely stunning.

"It's my tan." She laughed coquettishly.

"Why, I didn't know that coloured people tanned," Anthony said rather freely.

Before Isabella could agree, the girl coughed and spat wine across the table. Aidan, roused in anger, threw his father a menacing look and began fussing over the girl clumsily.

"Did I say something wrong?" Anthony asked, dabbing at his own face with his napkin.

"Slim is not *coloured*," Aidan said without any restraint.

"Darling, keep your voice down," Isabella said, "please!"

"Why should I?" he said. "I told you both that Slim is African-American."

"I'm sorry to have upset you, dear," Anthony said frowning. "But during the war, we openly used the word 'coloured' and no one objected to it."

"That was then," Aidan said. "This is now!"

"Sweetheart," the girl whispered. "Your father has apologised. It's an easy mistake. It happens." She glanced at Anthony and then at Isabella. "I'm so sorry for my bad manners," she said. "It's just that I was a bit taken aback by your statement about my skin tanning." She lowered her eyes. "All skin tans, Mr Chiltern. Skin is skin, you know."

Isabella had never seen her husband look more sheepish than at that moment. Clearly, he wanted to sink into his chair. Aidan, on the other hand, sat tall and beamed. Thank goodness the food arrived.

In between bites of the generously seasoned and sauced Italian food, Slim tried to patch things up, asking Anthony all sorts of questions about his years as a solicitor, and pretending to be totally engaged with his answers.

"How did you meet our Aidan?" Anthony asked.

"It's a funny story," she said smiling.

"We met at the Cannes Film Festival," Aidan chimed in and then clinked on his glass. "This is a good time to make a toast." They held up their glasses. "Not you, Slim," he said. "You're not allowed when you're being toasted." He took her hand, the one with the ring, and kissed it.

Isabella's heart threatened to hammer out of her chest and her ears filled with hot air.

"I'd like to thank the beautiful lady in my life for saying yes to starting a…" is all Isabella heard. She stuck a finger in her ear to try to release the pressure, but was unsuccessful. All she could do was watch the scene unfold. Anthony, overjoyed with the news— whatever it was—nudged her with his foot. She didn't understand his excitement. He knew full well that they could not allow Aidan to marry this girl, even if she was intriguing.

Desperately, she tried to contain herself and in a rush of heated anger, she felt her eardrums throbbing and then pop. She could hear again. "Have you told her about Andrew?" Isabella interrupted, instantly. "And have you told him about this news?"

"Of course I've told Slim about Andrew," Aidan said, looking agog. "He *is* my son. But why does Andrew need our news? I'll tell him in time."

"If he's going to have a *stepmother,*" Isabella emphasised the word, "don't you think he has a right to know?"

"A what?" Aidan said, looking at Slim admiringly. "Did Slim tell you something that she hasn't told me yet?"

The girl smiled and lowered her eyes.

"Darling, they're starting a fashion house together," Anthony said quietly. "Slim here is a fashion designer."

Relieved momentarily, Isabella soon flared up again emotionally. She didn't like the idea of the business arrangement either, but she'd take it any day over the personal one. "Congratulations to you both," she said sourly and raised her own glass to them.

"Hun, why don't you tell Mother about our little business," Aidan said and turned to his father. "What legal advice do you have for an old chap who's starting a new venture?"

Now Isabella had to think quickly and choose her words carefully. She needed to set the tone for the conversation; she would not allow the girl do so. "Do you have children, Slim?" she asked quickly.

"No," she said, hardly able to hold Isabella's stare. She fiddled with her hair incessantly, no longer the confident creature she had seemed. Suddenly, she seemed to long for something quite desperately. "Not yet! I've never married. I'm only thirty-seven. Nowadays, that's young."

Her talk didn't convince Isabella. "Why haven't you married?" she asked. "Surely, you've had your choice of men."

"I never met the right man," she replied, smiling curtly. "Until now, that is."

"Whatever makes you think Aidan is the right man?" Isabella asked sharply, feeling the irritation rise around her like a thick smoke, making her cough.

The girl seemed to be at a loss for words. She cleared her throat and reached for her water.

"Honestly, dear," Isabella said, "anyone can see that you two are like night and day."

"Will you excuse me," Slim said suddenly and stood. As she left the table, both Anthony and Aidan jumped up and watched her until she was out of the room.

"You didn't say anything to put Slim off, did you Mother?" Aidan asked.

"Of course not," Isabella answered. "She's a nice girl for a fling, darling."

"A *what?*" Aidan said harshly.

"I mean a friend," she said. "You wouldn't marry her and have children with her is all I am saying."

"Why not?" Aidan asked, scrunching his face.

"She's coloured," Isabella said flippantly.

"Don't use the word 'coloured' again, Mother!"

"Can we discuss this later, you two?" Anthony said. "We've had enough embarrassment for a year here today, don't you think?" He looked around.

"There's nothing to discuss," Aidan said and jumped up. "Actually, I have asked Slim to marry me, Mother! Father said you'd be this way. No wonder he asked me to give it some time."

"Excuse me?" Isabella said, glaring at her husband and then turning to Aidan. "Your father thinks you'd be insane to marry her. His words; not verbatim, but that about sums it up." Anthony rubbed his forehead and dropped his head in his hand

"Why, you sodden hypocrite!" Aidan said and stormed off.

Isabella didn't have the energy to try to stop him, nor did Anthony seemingly. She watched her son rush into the arms of the coloured girl, who had been returning from the toilet, presumably. As they talked animatedly in the doorway, Isabella grappled with her feelings. The odd emotion that had overcome her soon settled in her chest, making it burn violently. She didn't know whether it was anger or hurt, a combination of both, or something entirely different.

Her husband looked up slowly, his eyes so muddled that she could not wade through them. Then suddenly, she saw within them contempt. She somehow knew that Anthony was no more resigned to having Slim as a daughter-in-law than she was, but it was clearly more important to him to salvage his relationship with Aidan than his relationship with her. The last time, Aidan had not spoken to them for five long years, and Anthony had blamed her. But she refused to take responsibility for their son's socially unacceptable ex-wife.

However, as a result of the estrangement, Anthony had taken a mistress, and as if that hadn't been embarrassing enough, he had cavorted with her at the club. She had thought that was all behind them, but now she knew it wasn't. If only, like the lizard narrator in her novel, she had the power to create another past for herself, for all of them, surely it would make for a better future.

Suddenly, the coloured girl was standing at the table. Anthony stood and acknowledged her. Isabella continued sitting.

"I'm sorry that our first meeting has ended like this," she said quietly. Isabella looked away. The girl continued talking, her voice deep with remorse, if nothing else. "I must be a shock to you both."

"No, not at all," Anthony said softly. "Not at all."

"I can understand your concern for your son," she said softly, "but let me put your mind at rest. I love Aidan and I will do everything I can to make him happy."

Isabella turned and stared, and flinched at Anthony embracing the girl. Aidan was in the distance watching. She stood and stared at her son, who looked away. When Slim broke away from Anthony, she shot her a curt smile and turned away. She and Aidan left the restaurant holding hands Then Anthony turned to leave, too.

"I'll pay the bill and wait for you in the car," he said and walked off briskly.

With strangers ogling her, Isabella gathered her belongings and left the table. She'd lived long enough to wish desperately that she could change the past, but to know that wishing was futile. It was acting that was most useful. Thus, she would accept this girl, if only for show. If she had learned one thing over the years: that no one was quite what he, or she for that matter, seemed. Why on earth should she be any different?

When she got to the car, Anthony was standing outside smoking; something he had supposedly given up ages ago. She waved to him. He tossed the cigarette aside and opened the door for her.

"Off to the Lawns, shall we?" she said.

The Center of
Light

THE DEAD MAN SOARED ACROSS the stage and then took his bow with great theatrics. Even after Bebe caught his eye, he seemed to maintain the grace of a ballerina.

She, however, was anything but graceful. She couldn't even budge her body. Everyone else, including her husband Nick, hopped to their feet to show their appreciation for this American headliner.

All she could do was sit still and think about TC's eyes and how contented they were. She must have been the only one there who knew he had been dead for eleven years now.

Quietly, she wondered if anyone else had encountered the dead walking amongst the living, but felt afraid to admit it. Since moving to London ten years ago, she had seen three dead people: Maureen Fagan, a friend from high school, who had contracted the Aids virus from her husband and died years ago, was the first; Uncle Pap, her dad's brother, who had died a broken man after losing his job as a high school principal for something he did not do, was the second; now there was TC.

Though she had been sceptical about the first two sightings, she was certain about this one. But now that she thought about it, all three had something in common: their eyes. Before Uncle Pap, Maureen and TC had left the world, they had had vacant, desolate eyes. Each seemed to have lost something or given up on something. Upon returning to the earth, they each had translucent eyes that she could only describe as *satisfied*. Could they have returned for fulfilment?

Foolishly, she discussed her theory with Nick that night before going to sleep. She didn't mention TC, however. That was her secret. After eyeing her suspiciously, her husband asked if she should see the doctor again.

"Why?" she snapped, knowing full well why he thought this. After having had an ectopic pregnancy, which had led to an emergency hysterectomy, she had been diagnosed with depression. Sometimes Nick seemed to think she was a bit delusional, too. But she wasn't crazy; she was just tormented by secrets. That's all.

"Dead people don't return to earth." He stared at her. "We both know that. I really think you should talk it over with Harry."

"Forget it," she said and turned away.

"Anyway, isn't it unchristian to believe in reincarnation?"

She didn't answer, but to be honest, she didn't think so, and neither did the artist who rented space from her, who was also a Christian. When she told him about seeing a dead person from the past, he told her about a spiritualist called Alex that a friend had come across at a retreat. Apparently, Alex knew all about this type of thing.

At first, she pretended not to be interested, but after a few days, she asked how to get in touch. One morning after Nick had left the house, she made the call. When a woman answered and referred to The Centre of Light, Bebe apologised for calling the wrong number.

"Who are you looking for?"

"Alex," she admitted hesitantly.

"Alex isn't available," she said, "but if it's an appointment you need, I can help."

"Sure."

"When would you like to come?"

"As soon as possible," she said.

"We can see you on Friday, but that only gives you two days to prepare."

Bebe felt like hanging up. All she wanted was to discuss her theory. "Maybe I'll call you back."

"Up to you, dear," she said. "Alex books up quickly. This Friday there's a cancellation. After that, you'll have to wait a couple of months at least."

"Okay," Bebe said. "What do I need to do?"

"Bring some sort of information about the person in question; something tangible and relevant."

After agreeing to the appointment, she realized the meeting was in her neighbourhood. God, it all sounded spooky. Still she dressed and plotted how she would get something of TC's. That should not prove too difficult. As an artist, she was used to veering off the beaten path and collecting odd items.

Later that day, Bebe showed up at the theatre under the guise of wanting to work with TC and asked if they could put her in touch with him. The young man, on the desk told her to call TC's agent. That would have taken too long, so Bebe waited outside the stage door hoping to see him, but she missed him. The next day, however, as she was rushing to the door to stake it out, she saw him go into a nearby café and followed him there.

TC slid into the seat in the corner. There, he could have faded into the walls, similar to the colour of his clothes. He wore a mauve shirt, open at the chest, and slim jeans.

Bebe stood in the doorway, massaging the strap of her handbag, her fingers becoming raw. She wished he would look her way. Perhaps if they locked eyes, it would help. But as soon as the waitress brought his coffee and some sort of cake, he lowered his head and began eating. He took small bites the way she remembered.

Before she lost her nerve, Bebe hotfooted it over to where he sat.

"Hi, I'm an artist," she said. "Bebe Day."

He raised his head and looked at her. Unsurprisingly, his eyes conveyed that sheer sense of satisfaction she had seen the night of the musical. In his left ear, he had one sparkling pink earring. TC lowered his gaze and grabbed the back of his neck, something he always did when he was nervous. "How can I help?"

She slipped into the empty space across from him. "I'm doing a project on people in show business; people with alternative lifestyles," she said. "I'd like to ask you a few questions."

"Why me?" He looked up and smiled.

"You fit the bill," she said.

"Is this about homosexuals?" he asked, his voice deep and rich.

"No," she said, feeling a knot in her stomach. This man had stolen her virginity and her vitality, and was openly admitting to homosexuality.

Memories of their first meeting flitted through her mind. Her first job in the early '90s had been at her hometown newspaper as an artist, doing caricatures, sketches, and graphics... whatever they needed. She had also done art as a form of journalism. One day she came out of her cubicle to find a slim man sitting at the managing editor's desk.

She felt a shortness of breath as she had hurried past him, nearly tripping over the carpet. When she looked over her shoulder, she caught TC staring at her.

Neither of them was considered particularly pretty, not like most up-and-coming African-Americans in those days. Exotic, she guessed, was a better way of describing them both. Thanks to her Filipina mother, she had creamy skin and curly hair, but was plagued with a weight struggle. He was a waif-like creature with a cone head, but he had a big personality, which attracted people.

He had worked at the paper as a writer, but was now in between jobs, after a stint in Atlanta. Presently, he was staying locally with his mother, a well-to-do widow.

"Ms Day," TC said and reached out and touched her hand. She flinched. "Sorry," he said. He fiddled with his earring obsessively and then removed it from his ear. At last he put it on the table. "Are you all right?"

"Sure," she said. "Why did you ask if my project was about homosexuals?"

"Actually, I know your work. I just thought that you were about to expose the bible's lesbians and fags." He smiled wryly. "Shit! You do some pretty controversial stuff!"

Suddenly his phone chirped. He answered it and turned his head away and talked in a whisper. Bebe felt her heart pounding though she was happy for the opportunity to think about what she'd say. Admittedly, her work was a bit controversial, but it wasn't sacrilegious, even if her parents thought so. For years now, they had distanced themselves from her because of her interpretation of biblical women. Her most talked-about piece was a sculpture of Hagar, the Egyptian slave woman who had borne Abraham's first son, at his wife Sarah's arrangement. But when Sarah then became pregnant with her own son, she ousted the slave woman and her son, Ishmael. And to date, some believed they were the ancestors of the Arab nation. The bronze sculpture showed Hagar cradling Ishmael. She had also done a sculpture of a triumphant Sarah with her son, Isaac.

TC got off the phone, jumped up, dug a ten-pound note out of his pocket and threw it on the table. "I've gotta run," he said. "Good luck!"

He turned and fled without giving her a chance to protest. Still, she went after him. She needed something of his. "Hey, I have to get ..."

The waitress called out to her. "Ms, Ms … you left your earring." Bebe looked back to see the woman extending something to her. She took the earring and examined it. It was pink tourmaline. She smiled to herself and made her way home.

On her first date with TC, not only did Bebe get drunk, but also she lost her virginity. The daughter of a Baptist preacher and a pious mother, she still felt guilty about it. TC took her to his mother's mansion on the outskirts of town, cooked her steak and lobster and served two different kinds of wine. Since his mother was out of town, it was convenient for them to do whatever they pleased and for her to spend the night. Throughout the evening he regaled her with tales of his father, who had been a diplomat, and his beautiful mother, who had travelled all over the world with their only son. It was a world that she knew nothing of, and she loved hearing about it. In her own family, life was pretty local and restricted: her dad was the preacher; her mother the first lady; and she was their baby girl. Through TC, she escaped.

When they headed for his bedroom, Bebe's heart raced with anticipation as they stumbled into the room and fell onto the bed together. Earlier she had admitted to being a virgin, which seemed to arouse him further. In no time, they were between the sheets together. Sex had been a bitter-sweet ride for her: sweet as she clung to him; and bitter as she let go of her virginity.

As she lay in his arms, TC suggested that she use birth control pills. The next day she went to her doctor and did so. She was thankful for the pills, but would never forget the day her mother found them. Although that was more than twenty years ago, it felt like yesterday.

The Filipina woman had rushed into Bebe's room and hurled the packet at her. Bebe ducked, but the pills hit her on the head anyhow. As if that wasn't enough, her mother had slapped her across the face.

"But, Mum, I'm twenty-one," she said. "You have no right!"

"Sixteen, twenty-one, thirty-three... still a whore!" she yelled. "You opened your legs to a man without a wedding ring. Now if he doesn't marry you, you will always be another man's whore."

With the finesse of a magician, the woman snatched the curling tongs from the dresser and clenched its dangling cord. She brandished the plug with its silvery shiny prongs and shoved it into a socket. The tongs heated up.

"Electricity, connected forever: husband and wife."

True, Bebe had been raised to believe that sex was made for marriage. And if she was honest, she hoped

TC would marry her. But marriage was the last thing on his mind. He wanted fame and success. Thus after seeing her intensely for three months, he went to LA to become a PR man for the city's first African-American mayor, Tom Bradley.

"I can get a job at the *LA Times*," she'd said with excitement, having dreamt of moving to a major city.

"You're joking, right?" He laughed in her face. "What about a visit after I'm settled? I'll call you."

A month after he left, Bebe surprised him with a visit, telling her parents she had a job interview.

"What the f—k are you doing here?" he asked when she turned up at his office, though he cooled down later and made love to her throughout the night.

A month later, she found out she was pregnant. This time she knew he would marry her. How could he not? So she telephoned him with the news.

"But you were taking the pill," he said. "What happened?"

"I don't know."

"You're trying to trap me," he said in a vicious tone. Then he was silent. "I just landed this new job. Do you know who I am? I am Tom Bradley's f—ing right-hand man. I can't deal with this right now." He hurled a few more words at her and the final ones she would never forget. "I am *not* going to marry you!" Then he hung up on her.

Her life changed forever after that call.

The morning of Bebe's appointment with Alex, the sky was tawny, and the air was still stretching and yawning when she reached the High Street, but Camden was pretty much awake. A woman in a pastel designer dress and high heels parked her pink moped in front of a building that resembled a Rubik's cube. A young man wearing burnt orange bunny ears and a skin-tight suit walked with pizzazz, clinging to a bouquet of flowers.

Bebe stopped abruptly in front of The Centre of Light. It was a lighting shop, as its name suggested. Above its sign, a gaudy silver crown was mounted to each side, and in the middle hung the mother of chandeliers, leaves of glass pulled together with metal twigs. Thoughts of why she had never seen the place before scratched at her mind.

Still, she went inside. Only then did she remove the shawl from her shoulders and breathe more easily. She scrunched up the shawl and stuck it in her oversized bag. Hurriedly, she took her decorative chopstick from her bag and slipped it in her hair, securing a lose chignon.

Fanning herself to cool the fire in her chest, she moseyed around, pretending to look at chandeliers. Surprisingly, one caught her eye. Though it seemed smaller than the rest, its crystals sparkled in different colours. Suddenly, a scrawny shop assistant with blonde plaits approached her and asked if she wanted to buy a light.

She looked about the age Bebe's child would have been now; early twenties. Though she wasn't much to look at, she carried the tenderness of youth in her face.

"Does Alex work here by any chance?" Bebe asked.

"You're Debs," the girl said, smiling.

Bebe nodded, having given a fake name. Suddenly she realized the girl was gazing at her. She felt self-conscious, thinking of her tie-dyed oversized shirt, stone-washed jeans and Bo-ho trainers with tiny iridescent butterflies. "Is something wrong?" Bebe asked.

"No," she said, "but has anyone ever told you that you look like that cool Christian artist, Bebe Day?"

"Never heard of her," Bebe said, her heart racing. Why hadn't she realized that The Centre of Light was too close to her house on the Square? Maybe she ought to turn around and leave.

"You should look her up," she said. "You two could be twins."

"You know her?" she asked.

"No," the girl said. "Last week, at my college, we talked about her and her new piece, *Rebecca and the Twins*. They asked her to come and speak, but she said no. Apparently, she never speaks in public."

"Really?"

"Yeah, I think it's part of the mysticism."

Bebe didn't like public speaking for fear of having to talk about her past: her love–hate relationship with religion; or her abortion. She was thrilled when a tall straight-laced man came from the back and interrupted them.

"Gemma," he said in a posh English accent, "please send our guest in for her appointment."

"Sorry, Dad."

The man beckoned for Bebe to come through.

"You're Alex?" Bebe said in surprise. She had been expecting a menopausal woman with flowing silver hair and marks of wisdom in her face.

"Sorry to disappoint you," he said and led her into a small room. He pulled the door closed behind him and went ahead of her, sliding onto a low seat, almost a beanbag. He motioned for her to sit across from him on a similar one.

Bebe stood still, her eyes roaming the dull room. Through a dingy skylight, a slither of natural light forced its way in, but there were no lamps or chandeliers like in the shop. An oscillating fan swung around, throwing off stuffy heat.

At last Bebe looked at Alex. Now, he appeared rounder, like a Buddha, but a physically starved one. He watched her through squinted, brown eyes set in a wrinkled sunken face; a face that had traces of youth remaining. He must have been handsome at some point in his life.

"How did you find out about me?" He lifted the teapot, jiggled it and returned it to the small table that sat between them. She smelt roses.

"A friend," she said and dropped down on the stool. She removed the earring from her purse and held it in her hand. "I was told to bring something." She unfolded her fist.

Alex put on a tiny pair of glasses. He leaned over and took the earring and studied it. After staring at it for a while, he finally placed it on the table. "Most people are uncomfortable with this notion of reincarnation," he said, pouring tea into a tiny cup. When he offered her one, she declined.

"Yeah, my husband says it's unchristian."

He smiled and sipped his tea. His years seemed to come together underneath his eyes. "Well, it is an ancient doctrine of metaphysical belief," he said. "Some modern-day pagans and New Age movements believe it still happens."

"But not Christians," she said.

"You're a Christian," he said smiling, "and you believe you have seen the dead reincarnated."

"Yeah, I do," she said defensively. "Are you saying I don't?"

"Of course not, Ms Day," he said. Bebe interrupted him and asked how he knew her name. She had not told him. The friend of the artist she rented to must have told him.

"No," he insisted, "I don't know your colleague or his friend."

"Then, how do you know who I am?" she questioned.

"It comes with the territory," he said and smiled curtly.

"I see," she said.

"I know you have taken great risks to come here," he said. "Your husband doesn't know you're here, nor does your vicar, I gather."

Nervously, she fiddled with the chopstick in her hair.

"Not to worry. Your visit is confidential," he said.

"Good," she said. "How do I know I can trust you? I mean, I don't know anything about you. Is Gemma truly your daughter? Are you raising her alone? And if so, why? How did you become a spiritualist? What's your story?"

He laughed softly. "You're not here for me," he said. "All you need to know is that I can help you. That's all."

"Fine," she snapped. "Was it TC that I saw?"

"It was TC," he said. "It was also Maureen and your Uncle Pap."

"So you know about all three of them?" Bebe asked. He nodded. "Why did they come to see me? Well, why did TC come to see me? That's really what I want to know!"

"He needed to," Alex said softly. He leaned back and propped his leg on his knee. His withered eyes turned dreamy.

"Why?" she asked.

"He needed to satisfy his soul," he said. "In actuality, it was his soul that sought you."

"I don't understand," she said.

"Let me explain," he said. "Think of the soul as a fire that burns bright and will only die down when there is no oxygen left in it. Even when it appears to be snuffed out, it smoulders."

Bebe held the image in her mind. Her throat felt dry. She poured herself a cup of his tea. Taking a swallow, she thought of her suspicions about TC, that he was gay: the way he dressed; how he walked; his gestures. And her own closet gay cousin had met TC once and had warned her that the man was too much like him. Of course, TC had denied it all.

"He was gay, wasn't he?" She asked, thinking how difficult it must have been for TC as a black man in the South to come clean, especially one who came from an upper-crust family. "He never lived it out, so his soul has returned to fulfil itself?"

"That could very well be." he said, "but I sense that his soul had an overarching goal; this was a part of it."

Bebe remembered how much TC had desired fame.

"In any case, don't confuse his soul's return to earth with why he came to see you."

Bebe rubbed her chest. It still hurt to think about what had happened after TC had hung up on her. Since she could not face her parents or even a girlfriend, she had had an abortion that had been so botched that her uterus had been irreparably damaged. She hadn't known that until her ectopic pregnancy. As it happened, however, a few years after TC had dumped her, the bastard had married again and had another child. When she first met him, he'd been divorced with a daughter. Thinking of it, her eyes watered.

"You think he came to apologize?" she said.

"That's part of it," Alex said, "but I'd take it further."

Bebe eyed him curiously.

"After your abortion, you were so disillusioned that you left the world that you knew and adopted a new cold, steely one."

It was true; Bebe had heeded her grandmother's advice and carried her love in her hand, not her heart, so that she could be ready to throw it away at any time. She wasn't even sure if she truly loved Nick. She had married him with the idea of having a family, and only when she'd had the ectopic pregnancy did she find out that this would not be possible.

She had long stopped sleeping with her husband and only now and again went out with him, like the night they had seen TC in the play. Most days she didn't even feel like getting out of bed. It was her work that kept her going, because in it she could invent happy endings for the women and live vicariously through them.

"Now that TC has satisfied his soul," he said, "he wants to help you do the same thing."

"That's not possible." Bebe stared at Alex. "Because of him, I don't even have a uterus. I can't have a family."

"Is it your virginity," Alex asked, "that your soul craves? If this is so, why did you have so many men after TC?"

Bebe lowered her gaze.

"Is it a baby that your soul craves?" Bebe did not answer. "If this is so, why don't you adopt? Your husband has suggested it many times."

"I don't know what my soul craves," she said, confused.

"Then you need to find out," Alex said softly. "And once you do, feed it, and only then can you live a fulfilled life."

"So you're saying a soul can be satisfied in life?"

"Yes," he said. He had taken off his glasses. He picked up the earring and massaged it between his slim fingers. "In which case, there is no need to return."

Bebe thought of her parents, and Nick. She had desperately wanted to give them what they wanted, especially her mother. But nothing would satisfy her mother, except for going back all those years and marrying as a virgin.

"Ms Day, three sightings are rare," Alex said, bringing her out of her thoughts. "There has to be a message for you. Each person died unfulfilled. Maybe they are each saying that there is no need for you to let this happen to you. Perhaps that is the message here." Alex placed the earring back on the table.

"Am I dying?"

"I am not suggesting that there is something imminent about to happen," Alex said. "But I am saying you must rethink how you live your life. Who are you living for?"

Bebe felt anxious to leave now, to think things through on her own.

He stood. "I wish you well, Ms Day."

"Thank you," she said and glimpsed the earring. "Can I keep it?"

"It's yours," he said. "TC left it for you."

Bebe reached for the earring, but somehow knocked it to the floor. She slipped off her seat to retrieve it. By the time she looked up, Alex was gone. She eased up and looked around, and called out to him. But he was nowhere to be found. She stayed as still as she could, holding her fist close to her heart. Now the fan produced cool air.

She hadn't even paid Alex, she thought, dropping the earring in her purse. In the shop, she looked around for Gemma, but there was no sign of her either. There was, however, a stocky lady who appeared out of nowhere. She wore tiny glasses and a lavish decorative comb in her hair.

"Are you all right dear?" she said. "Looking for anything special today?"

"I'd like to pay," she said.

The woman smiled quizzically. "Oh, so you've chosen a light?"

Bebe opened her mouth to explain, but then thought better of it.

"I'll have that smaller chandelier over there," she said, pointing to where she thought she'd seen the one with the sparkling crystals. She had no idea what it cost. She and the woman went to the area. It was no longer there.

"What about this one?" the woman said of a gaudy one, similar to the one above the sign outside.

Suddenly, Bebe felt overwhelmed. She thanked the lady for her time and rushed out of the shop into the daylight. Hurriedly, she walked towards her house. As she took in the fresh air, she began to wonder if she was delusional. Maybe she would talk to the doctor, after all.

In the meantime, she knew one thing for sure, that she had TC's earring and because of it, she had a new perspective on fulfillment. In her gut, she felt a deep hunger. She didn't know what it was for, but she had a strong will to find out.

Autumn

"Autumn is the mellower season and what we lose in flowers, we more than gain in fruits."

~Samuel Butler

The Storm

Before the storm

THAT AFTERNOON WHEN THE WIND began to howl angrily, Mama Bradley was sitting in her rocking chair on the front porch, finishing up her first grandchild's blanket. She looped the last bit of yarn through a hole and tightened it. Now all she had to do was finish the one for the second baby, but she needn't worry. She had nearly two months to do that.

For now, she ought to get inside. No sooner had she gathered her belongings and rose to make haste to the front door than the chairs toppled behind her. Then the rain came spilling out of the sky, bringing with it a dull darkness.

Inside, she almost bumped into her seventeen-year-old pregnant daughter. Ruby hugged herself, her eyes wild with fear. It was clear that the gal feared the weather terribly, but Mama, a retired midwife with more than thirty years of experience, saw something else in her eyes, too—the dread of giving birth. But she didn't need to worry about that yet. Doc Phillips said she had seven weeks to go.

"Get away from this door, gal," Mama scolded, feeling the old house rattle underneath her feet. Ruby stood still, trembling. Mama bolted the door, and as soon as she turned around, lightning flung a psychedelic line between her and Ruby and snuffed the power out.

Mama took her daughter by the arm and began making her way through the darkness. Counting under her breath, she didn't make ten before thunder clapped, shaking the house again.

"Son," she called out, going toward Matt's old bedroom. "Get the lamps, the candles."

Soon Matt was standing before them, his pregnant wife beside him. Her arm was draped loosely around his neck. In his free hand, he held on to a suitcase.

"Juanita ain't doing so well," he said, his voice urgent. "If we're going to make it to the hospital, we've got to go now."

"Hospital," Mama said, feeling her daughter's grip on her arm. She reached over and took her daughter-in-law's chin, looked into her eyes. Then she glanced at her drooping stomach. Lord have mercy. This couldn't be. "Did your mucus plug come, chile?"

Juanita nodded. "But I haven't had contractions to speak of until about an hour or so ago, so I didn't worry, but now the pain is coming faster and sharper," she said, her voice trailing off.

"My plug came, too," Ruby said tearfully.

"Mama," Matt said, "we got to go." He looked over at his sister. "You see about Ruby. I'm taking Nita to the hospital."

"Take her to my birthing room," Mama said confidently, although she had not delivered a baby in more than five years. Doc Phillips had said Juanita had three weeks to go, but from what Mama could tell, he was wrong. True, some women were still two weeks or so after the mucus plug, but others were ready then, especially those that showed physical signs in the neck and stomach, for instance. As for Ruby, she didn't really believe her.

Matt eyed her suspiciously. "Mama," he said firmly, "we need the doctor."

"Ain't no time," she said. "You gonna have to trust me, son. My gut don't fool me about the timing. Juanita is ready."

"Matt," Juanita whispered. "Do what your mother says. Please, listen to her."

Quickly, Matt moved, picking up his wife and carrying her in his arms. Mama stood still until Ruby tugged her arm. She complained that she felt her baby kicking and she was in pain, too. This morning, Mama had made her run chickens. Somebody had to do it, and she was the best candidate. Now she was pretending like this had put her into labor. Mama wouldn't hear of it; she did more than run chickens when she was with child.

She moved off toward the birthing room, her daughter clinging to her. On the way there, Mama petitioned the Lord silently.

"What do you want from me, Lord? Whatever it is, you got to be clear. And you've got to guide me," she said repeatedly. "Help me, Lord. Help me. I can't do this without you."

In the room, Mama moved with more energy than she thought she had, fluffing the sheets on each twin bed and patting them down. Sneezing, she thought of weevils, moths, all the things that might have been in the sheets, but she didn't have time to look for better ones. She had to gather up some towels, as many as she could.

Meanwhile, Juanita rested, sighing and moaning, on the old sofa, and Ruby paced the floor, grunting. Matt lit the candles and the kerosene lamps and started a fire in the old fireplace. He put a couple of dishpans of water on it to heat up. He stuck an old bucket underneath the leaking ceiling, too. She didn't even have to tell him these things; he knew what to do. She knew, too, but, Lord, she was nervous.

The sounds of the storm crept up through the bottom of her feet and moved all the way to the tips of her fingers, making them tingle. She eyed her old hands. Even the darkness couldn't mask the wrinkles spiderwebbing over them. Still, she steadied herself and got to work.

When each woman was in a bed, Mama laid arthritic hands on them one at a time, right at the base of the neck. It was there that the line formed. Doc Phillips said there was no such thing. Maybe it wasn't for him. But for her, this line was often like a thick, soft rope. She wasn't surprised when she felt the chunkiness in Juanita's neck, but when she felt the thickness in Ruby's, a shock ran through her body. Then she knew she was in the eye of perhaps the biggest storm of her life.

During the storm

Working in the dimly lit room, she remembered it all, the intermittent cries rising around her, the thick smell of salves almost taking her breath away, and the intensity of eyes watching her. All she could do was work to an emotional detachment to keep from falling apart. She coached both women to take deep breaths and checked their cervix for dilation. It was going to be a long night, she could tell. Ruby screamed when she stuck her finger up her, said she was trying to hurt her. The girl sprung up in the bed. Mama then rubbed her back intensely. Meanwhile, she told Matt to turn Juanita to the side and rub her back. Her daughter-in-law cried pitifully.

Then suddenly, Juanita's cries turned into screams, sounds that were sharp and urgent. Mama left Ruby

staring into darkness and turned to Juanita's bed.
Immediately, she saw that her water had broken and
that it was stained with blood. Matt looked at Mama
beseechingly. Thank God, he couldn't see into her
worried eyes; she had been born cross-eyed. Some
said it was a plague, but for her it was a blessing.
It had made delivering bad news bearable. She was not
prepared for a medical emergency.

"Do something, Mama!" he said.

She grabbed a towel and wadded it up and pressed
it to her daughter-in-law"". She had to stop the
bleeding. Juanita seemed to flinch and sputter out.

"Mama, do something, please!" Matt said. "You
can't just let her die."

"I'm doing all I can," she said weakly. "Ain't
nothing more I can do."

"Matt!" Juanita cried. "Matt, get the doctor. Help
me, please!"

He looked from his wife to his mother.

On some level, Mama knew that whatever would
be would be, long before any doctor could arrive.
"Ain't no time for that," Mama said sorrowfully.
"The baby is coming, son."

"I need a doctor," Juanita moaned. "I need a doctor."

Mama's heart felt heavy. She could see the blood
coming through the towel. In all of her days, she had

never been in such a predicament. She looked into her son's frustrated face. He hovered over his wife, gazing at her pitifully. "I'm going to fetch Doc Phillips," he said, his dark lips trembling.

"It's might stormy out there, son!" Mama said. "It will all be over by the time you make to town and back."

"I got to try!" He raised his voice. "I can't stand here and watch my wife and child die." Without giving her a chance to protest, he tore away.

"Get your boots!" Mama called after him, still holding a towel to Juanita. "Trust in the Lord, son. Trust in the Lord."

"You can't let him go out there!" Ruby cried out. "He ain't gonna make it in all that rain."

"Hush up," Mama said. "Just hush up, now!"

Ruby scooted up in the bed. Mama felt her gaze. Then Ruby flung her legs to the side of the bed.

"What are you doing, gal?" Mama said. "You ain't fit for nothing. Lay your narrow tail down."

"I can't lay down," she cried. "My back's hurting."

"Matt," Juanita murmured and rolled her head to the side in sorrow. "Where's Matt?"

"You sent him out in the storm!" Ruby said, wailing. "And Mama let him go."

Juanita grabbed Mama's hand and squeezed it lightly.

"Hush, gal!" Mama hollered over to Ruby. "And stay in that bed. Your brother is going to make it. He knows the Lord."

"You know as well as I do that the best of drivers don't have a chance on that slippery road. He'll end up knocked out in a ditch."

"The ole pickup's headlights will become his eyes," Mama said quietly. "He's a good driver. Been driving a tractor since he was ten."

She patted Juanita's hand and prayed silently. God knows she hated for Matt to go, but she couldn't stop him, could she? She knew that no normal person could see easily during a storm on the Acres. Darkness so black that it took special eyes to bore through it. But with the help of the Lord, Matt would develop extraordinary sight. He had to, even if the trip would be in vain.

"He ain't going to make it!" Ruby cried, wriggling her way back down in the bed. "Ya'll know he ain't gonna make it!"

Ruby's voice faded into the background, as Mama leaned over and whispered to her daughter-in-law. "Don't pay Ruby Nell any mind," she said. "She ain't but a child herself. She don't know what she talking about. Matt is going to be fine, and so are you. And my granddaughter, too."

"Granddaughter," Juanita whispered.

"Mm, hmm," Mama said. "I know by your stomach."

Mama closed her eyes briefly and prayed the most selfish prayer she had prayed. She asked God to spare her son, his wife, and their unborn child. She said nothing of her daughter. Right then, she couldn't stand the gal. Had she not been such a whore, they would not be in this position. On account of her getting pregnant out of wedlock, Matt left a good job in the city and came home to help out on the farm. Ruby wouldn't be much help no more, and they had to earn a living somehow. Since her husband Matt Senior had died, she had been farming, herself.

Mama checked Juanita's bleeding, which seemingly had slowed down, maybe even stopped. Still, she pressed another towel close to her and forced herself to check on Ruby.

Her daughter's pulse was fast. Also, she was hot with fever. Mama looked at the fall of her belly; it was low. The pressure had to be unbearable. How could the doctor have been so wrong?

"Did your water break already?" She asked Ruby.

The girl nodded.

"You got to be hurting some kind of terrible," Mama said angrily.

The girl nodded, crying. "I knew I shouldn't have run those chickens. I knew it."

Mama didn't rise to the bait. She touched Ruby's forehead, disturbed by her clammy skin. Quickly, she checked her dilation again. Lord have, mercy, it was time. Meanwhile, Juanita grunted, causing Mama to turn and take a quick look at her. She couldn't see any real change in the baby's movement. She pushed a cloth drenched in salves underneath her daughter-in-law's nose. This would hold her long enough for Mama to get the baby out of Ruby. Mama went about her work.

After the storm

The dead baby came three weeks early and the live one a whole seven weeks. Both were girls, one's eyes stitched together, her mother's fluids sealing them. The other's were slits that barely opened at first, but when they did, they seemed to flutter to the candlelight.

Mama sat slumped over an old dishpan. The candlelight bouncing off its tarnished color made it appear soft. But it felt hard, making ridges on her arms where they rested on it. She lifted her head slightly and looked at her hands, still tainted with blood, blood of her daughter and daughter-in-law, her grandchildren.

She plunged her hands into the water and looked around for a clean towel to dry them, but not a one was in sight. So she took off her head rag and wiped her brow and then dried her hands. She laid the rag aside.

Then she waited in the still of the room, listening to the sounds of the leaking ceiling and the ticking

clock. Plop. Plop. Plop. Tick tock. The bucket that
Matt had left to catch the water would soon be full.
And from the sounds of the old battery-operated wall
clock, it would give all it had soon. She looked at it.
Two hours had gone. Thoughts of her son knocked
out in a ditch scratched at the back of her mind. She
swallowed hard and tried to push the thoughts away.

But if it was so, all she had left now was the gal and
her baby. Matt's wife lay limp, barely holding on to
life. Surely Juanita would die, too, if her husband
already had. And at her feet was their stillborn baby,
bundled up in the tricolor blanket Mama had finished
hours earlier.

Hesitantly, she looked at the twin bed where Ruby
lay. She faced the wall, her hair sprouting like a large
bush. Though her baby had put up a hollering after
she was born, the gal hadn't so much as looked at her.
She didn't even hold her, just turned away. Mama
cleaned up the little miracle and wrapped her in an old
tattered blanket.

Mama knew better than most that God knew best,
but the burning in her chest forced her to question
Him. Why did he sacrifice her son? Even if he
had made it through the storm, he had been dealt
a horrible hand. He had lost his first wife to an
aneurism, and this wife had already had two
miscarriages before this loss. A weaker woman than
most black women Mama had attended to, Juanita did
not suffer well at all. She had already said that if this

pregnancy was a failure, she wasn't trying anymore. She wanted to adopt.

Mama didn't have the words to explain how she felt about adoption. Everybody who went down that route, to her mind, ended up with a deformed child or a wayward one. But what she thought didn't matter. It was what Matt thought that concerned her the most. He wanted his own child to keep the Bradley lineage going. Mama understood that. God knows she did. What would he do if faced with this new problem? He had already turned to drinking and smoking. She saw the evidence in his bloodshot eyes and on his dark lips. She wasn't blind. Cross-eyed but not blind.

The other question that plagued her was why God had celebrated Ruby, so to speak. She could just as easily have had the stillbirth. Wouldn't that have been better? She didn't want the baby anyhow, and she didn't even have a husband. The rascal that made her pregnant blew into town with the Civil Rights movement and opened her nose wide. She told Ruby to stop hanging around with him. And then one day she caught them humping and moaning in the barn. Took all she could not to shoot him. Good thing she knew the Lord, because if she hadn't, instead of firing into the air, she would have killed him.

He wasn't a bit of good, just like she suspected. He jumped into his britches, swearing he was going to marry Ruby but hightailed it out of town. They hadn't seen him since.

Why had it turned out like this? Suddenly, her heart burned so intensely she felt tears trickle down her face, then her neck and into her bosom. She heard herself sobbing softly.

"Mama, why are you crying?" Ruby's scraggly voice frightened her.

"Shush," Mama said, trying to dry up her tears. Ruby was not used to her crying. Even at Matt Senior's funeral, Mama held back her tears. She threw a glance toward Juanita.

"Matt's baby dead, isn't she?" Ruby asked in a whisper. From where Mama sat, she could see her daughter shivering, her blanket moving. So skinny, Ruby was always cold, even with the fireplace throwing off heat.

Mama got up and grabbed a throw from the old sofa and threw it over Ruby. She nodded to answer her question. As she started to turn away, Ruby caught her hand and gripped her fingers tightly, something neither of them was used to.

The gal's gaze was discomforting, even if it was that of her little girl who had fallen off her tricycle and scraped her knee on the pavement, and not that of the woman who had stood between them for the past couple of years. Mama had forgotten how pretty she was. The longest eyelashes and thickest eyebrows she ever set eyes on.

"Matt's coming home," Ruby whispered. "He'll be here in a little while."

Mama snatched her hand away and stared intensely. "You sound like somebody done heard from the Lord."

"I saw it as clear as day," she said softly, wriggling up in the bed. She was much stronger than she should have been. "Juanita is gonna be all right, too."

All Mama could do was look and listen. She guessed the Lord could use anybody. Anybody. "What else did you see?"

"They had a little girl," she said, smiling. "A little girl who looked like Matt."

Mama rubbed her chest, trying to calm it down.

"How does she look Mama?" Ruby asked.

"You mean Matt's girl?" she answered softly. "A sleeping beauty. She didn't make it, Ruby. I thought you understood that."

Ruby brought her hand up to her eyes. "I know," she said, wiping her eyes. "But they got a little girl." She looked to the foot of the bed where her baby lay.

"Hush up," Mama said. "You don't know what you're talking about."

"Yes, I do," Ruby said and asked if she could see her baby.

Suddenly, light flooded the room, iridescent colors streaming from the bulb merging into a burst of white light. Mama's eyes searched her daughter's youthful face. Though she hesitated, she picked up the baby and carefully passed her to Ruby. She watched her daughter hold the infant loosely and study her.

"You look like your daddy," she said softly.

Mama glanced at her grandchild. She didn't look like that rascal at all. She looked like Ruby had spit her out. Ruby and Matt both looked like their father had made them in his own image. So caught up in her thoughts, Mama jumped at Ruby's sharp whisper.

"Mama! Take her—Matt will be here soon." She extended the baby to her.

"She's yours," Mama said. "You've got to learn to attend to her. You can't undo what the Lord has done."

"You can't, either," she said firmly. "Now take her and give her to Juanita. Matt will be here in a little while."

"Baby, you don't know what you're saying." Then Mama jumped at the rumbling of the pickup truck driving into the yard.

"I told you Matt would be here soon." Ruby stared at her intensely and handed the baby to her. "Give her to Juanita now."

Cradling the baby and staring at her daughter, Mama felt weak in the knees. As much as she wanted Matt to have a baby, she knew that no mother was expected to make such a sacrifice. "It doesn't have to be this way, daughter," she whispered. "You might change your mind."

"It's not my decision," Ruby said firmly. "Not yours, either. Go on, Mama, do it!" She looked toward the door. "Matt will be here soon."

Mama didn't know from where her strength came, but she somehow moved quickly and put the baby girl beside Juanita. The woman stirred as if she knew she had been given life, but she kept sleeping.

Then Mama picked up the dead infant and moved away from the bed. As the sound of footsteps neared the birthing room, she remembered her prayers, asking the Lord to tell her loud and clear what was required of her. She had asked him to guide her, to help her, and to save Matt.

Still holding the dead infant, she sat on the side of the bed, feeling her daughter's young body tremble. When Matt tore into the room with Doc Phillips, Mama pointed him toward his wife's bed.

Clarinet Moments

AFTER THIS MORNING'S MEETING TO close the biggest deal of his life, Geoffrey Grant will finally be able to call himself a successful man. No longer will his countless failures and disgraces be etched into his mind. Tying his tie, he glances in the mirror and smiles. When his Blackberry rings, he answers on speakerphone.

"Geoff Grant here," he says, his voice high in spirit.

"Mr Grant, it's Mr Coster from the Royal Marsden."

Geoff's fingers stop working on his tie. He looks around the room, picks up the phone and puts it to his ear. No need, however. He is alone. His wife Nina has pushed off to a board meeting and the children are at school. Their nanny and housekeeper, Sylvia, is away in Lithuania for a week.

"What can I do for you?" he asks hesitantly.

"I have your pathology report here," he says, "the results from both the fine-needle aspiration and the mammogram. I'd like to see you this morning to discuss them."

Geoff moves to his bed and drops down on the edge of it. He plucks at his trousers. "This morning?" he questions. "Aren't I scheduled to see you at the London Clinic next week? Didn't we fix that in your diary?"

"We did," he says, "but I'm afraid I can't make that consultation. I've been called away to South Africa, and I'd like to see you before I go."

Geoff feels a rush of heat in his face. He rubs his forehead. Though he doesn't particularly like Mr Coster, a short South African with scattered hair and sharp eyes, he trusts him because he is frank.

"What have you found?" Geoff asks.

"I'm afraid it's invasive breast cancer," Mr Coster says quietly.

The news hits Geoff with such force that the heat in his face spreads like fire through his body. Upon reflection, he shouldn't have been stunned, having experienced soreness in his armpit for some time now and a bloody discharge from his nipple. Still he can't believe he has breast cancer.

"Mr Grant?" the man calls out.

"Yes," Geoff says, loosening his tie. "It's not what I expected to hear."

"Why don't you come in this morning and we'll talk about it," the consultant says.

"This afternoon," Geoff says, eyeing his briefcase. "I have a meeting this morning that I absolutely cannot miss. I'll come to the London Clinic."

"I'm in theatre this afternoon." Mr Coster's voice goes up an octave. "This morning, 9.30 a.m., at the Royal Marsden."

"I can give this thirty minutes. That's all I have for it. I'll call in on the way to my 10.30."

Geoff rings off, drops the phone on the bed and rips off his yellow-striped tie. He tosses it aside. Overheated, he makes his way to the en suite and splashes cold water on his face. While lifting his left arm, he feels the soreness in his armpit. He towel-dries his face and goes back to the bedroom.

Sitting on the edge of his bed again, he wonders what in the world he is supposed to tell Peter, his business partner. He can't miss the signing of the deal. He *won't* miss it. Suddenly, it occurs to him to tell him the truth. Surely, this is enough reason to delay the deal signing? Geoff picks up the phone and then thinks better of this approach. He knows better than anyone that the truth is never the best course in the long run. It fucks people up, imprisons them in abysmal darkness. He should know.

He was a teenager when he had first learned this hard lesson. As if his father's sudden death of a heart attack hadn't been tragic enough, it had dug up family secrets that had been long buried. As it was, the Grants were not only Jewish, but because his father had escaped the Holocaust when other family members hadn't, he had detached himself from his heritage. According to his long-distant cousin, who had had a similar experience, the humiliation slowly turned into indignation over the years. It was too much to own. Renunciation was his only way to survive.

That revelation had totally screwed Geoff up. He went on a rampage to destroy himself and even when he came out on the other side, he competed for everything and with everybody, even years later. For instance, when he first met Nina, who was also an ambitious banker, he knew he wanted to be with her, to stare endlessly into her intense green eyes and talk beyond the superficial for hours on end. She was the most engaging creature he had ever met. Still, he competed with her forcefully, risking losing her quite often. But she hung in there, and about three years into their marriage, he seemed to wash out career-wise as far as banking was concerned, while Nina rode the biggest wave of her life. The morning after he had lost the job that would have made him or broken him, Nina had made passionate love to him and afterwards asked if he felt threatened by her success. Foolishly, he told her the truth. Instantly, Nina changed. Over the coming weeks, he saw her transform from a woman who passionately valued her work to another who thought of nothing else but having children.

And when he couldn't deliver, she insisted on going to see a fertility specialist. He'd never forgive her for that, because had she *not* done that, he might have never known that he was odd... genetically, that is. He had a rare condition called Klinefelter's Syndrome, meaning he was born with an extra female chromosome, making him XXY and XY. Sure, he had noticed that he had more breast tissue than other boys, but he had put it down to being a bit heavier in those days. Also, the family doctor hadn't said anything about it. He was fine with a slightly bulkier chest, but the revelation that he couldn't have children because of the condition had such an impact on his manhood that he and Nina had agreed to have her fertilized clandestinely. No one else knew apart from the specialists who had been involved.

Though they'd been married for seventeen years, they stayed away from the truth as much as possible nowadays. They both spoke and behaved as if he had really fathered their children. And maybe he had somehow. Anyhow, he hadn't told his wife about the breast cancer symptoms, let alone that he had been seeing Mr Coster.

He shakes his head, coming out of his thoughts and rings his business partner, his heart thumping with dread. Relieved when his voicemail picks up, Geoff fabricates a story about his nine-year-old son having a frightful virus. Since Sylvia is away and Nina is already in a meeting, he has to collect him. He'll miss their pre-meeting but he'll make the 10.30, come hell or high water.

Geoff shuts the phone off, gets up from the edge of the bed and shoves it in the inside pocket of his suit jacket, still hanging on the back of the chair. After taking a dark blue tie from his rack, he stands in front of the mirror, tying it. His face, now flushed, is damp and his chest wet, too, as are his underarms. His shirt sticks to him. He glances at his watch, grabs his jacket and heads out the door.

Soon he is on his Yamaha motorbike, riding to the nearby Royal Marsden. He could have walked there in fifteen minutes, but he will use the bike to make his meeting.

At 9.30 a.m. precisely, he goes into the hospital and bypasses the waiting room. As he is about to knock on Mr Coster's door, a nurse opens it. She eyes him suspiciously, but moves aside for him to go in. Inside, Mr Coster is fiddling with the old window. He opens it and turns around, gesturing for Geoff to have a seat across from his desk. The nurse leaves the room promptly.

Geoff shuffles in his chair while Mr Coster studies the pathology report. He can't remember ever feeling so worked up as an adult, not even when he had lost the top job, or when he had learned that he had Klinefelter's.

'There must be a mistake," Geoff says angrily.

"Mr Grant, your mammogram and your needle aspiration were conclusive," he says. "This must be shocking news, but unfortunately around 300 to 400 men in the UK are diagnosed each year."

"I see," Geoff says, lowering his eyes. "Is this a rare type of cancer?"

"Invasive breast cancer of no type accounts for about 75% of all breast cancers."

Geoff rubs the back of his neck, listening to the man explain the details of this cancer. "It's stage 2B," he says… or something. The lump in his breast is fairly large. Also, the cancer is a grade two, which means the cells are growing quickly.

"What's the prognosis?" Geoff glances up.

"It's fair," Mr Coster says. "You have an 80% five-year survival rate."

Geoff makes a fist and exhales into it. "What exactly does that mean?"

"Out of one hundred people diagnosed with breast cancer, eighty are likely to be alive after five years. Having said this, you must remember that every case is unique and we can't say for certain what will happen to you. In any case, we'll need to start treatment right away."

Geoff feels a lump in his throat. Although the man's bedside manner is not desirable, he appreciates his straightforwardness. "What does that entail?"

"A mastectomy," he says, "and…"

Geoff interrupts. "Surely, there's another way."

"Mastectomy is the most common treatment for men with breast cancer," he says. "Also, we'll do a lymph node removal from your underarm to find out if any of the tissue there contains cancer. This will tell us whether you will need chemotherapy."

"Chemo," Geoff says quietly.

"Our aim is to remove the cancerous tissue and destroy any cells that we don't remove."

"Why am I one of those 300 or other men that you mentioned earlier? Why me?" Geoff shuffles in the chair, feeling the lump in his throat swell. "It doesn't add up. I have no history of any type of cancer that I know of, and don't have any other risk factors, do I? I'm otherwise healthy, wouldn't you agree?"

"Cancer is complicated," Mr Coster says. "While you are an otherwise healthy individual, you do have Klinefelter's, and men with Klinefelter's are about twenty times more likely to get breast cancer than the average man."

Geoff's face tingles. He has not come to terms with being born with an extra female chromosome, and he probably never will. He's heard enough. He gets up and heads towards the door.

Before he exits, Mr Coster reminds him to make an appointment with a nurse specialist or some sort on the way out, and to bring his wife along. There, they can get all their questions answered and also arrange for his treatment to begin.

Outside, he stumbles down the steps and plods towards home, not remembering his motorbike until he feels soft rain. He walks slowly, feeling his chest tighten and his eyes fog up.

In his Chelsea basement, slumped on the floor, Geoff has drunk nearly a bottle of wine. He puts his glass aside. Though he no longer feels overheated, he feels muggy inside. He unbuttons his shirt and glances at his watch. 10:42 a.m. He's late for the meeting, but he doesn't care. Now, he only cares about one thing: quietening his thoughts. He picks up his clarinet from the floor beside him and stares at it. He has had the same instrument since he was six. And since he was fourteen, he has been a part-time professional clarinettist, but not because he loves playing the instrument or wants to be famous, but because he needs to play it, in a quest for a peace that only playing the clarinet can give him.

He first came across this fact after learning about his family's past. For weeks, if not months, his rampage included drinking, smoking, doing drugs and having sex with older girls, some women. He had a one-off with a boy, too. He hasn't told anyone this. Not even Nina. After it happened, he locked himself in his room for hours, cogitating. At some point, his mother came and started banging on the door, pleading with him. The pounding hurt his ears, but he refused to let her in. He couldn't believe it when she started shouting about the past, right through the door. He sat frozen on the floor, hugging his knees as she disclosed unthinkable circumstances.

"Don't allow your father's past to destroy you, Geoffrey," she said. "Please! Your father was a little boy…seven; a boy when it happened." She went quiet and then spoke again. "Just before soldiers broke into their home, his own father shoved him into a cupboard and made him promise to stay quiet, no matter what. In the next few minutes, he heard his mother and teenage sister's shrill cries and his father's screams and sobs. He even heard a gunshot." Her voice trembled. "That boy, your father, was traumatized. He never saw his family again, Geoffrey. How could you expect him to get over that? How?"

Geoff remembered wanting to speak out, if only to tell her to shut up, but he'd sat stunned. In those days, he didn't even have a record player. His parents had been strict disciplinarians about him focusing only on his clarinet.

"Although his guilt and shame turned him bitter," she said quietly, "he made certain you didn't see that side of him, Geoffrey." She raised her voice again. "If his so-called cousin had not shown up here at his funeral, you would not be cross with him. He was a good father, Geoffrey; a good father. He spared you the wretched truth."

His mum's crying had tortured him. He remembered aching all over and being desperate to shut her up. Suddenly, his own larger-than-life problems merged with his father's, causing him deep pain. He noticed his clarinet on the desk. He crawled over to it and took it to his lips. Without hesitation, he blew into the mouthpiece like there was no tomorrow, and somehow discovered unprecedented solace. The more he played the instrument, the more he felt whole. It was better even than any lovemaking or drug that he had encountered in his teenage life. He had no memory of what music he had played. It didn't matter. What mattered was the sensation he had got from bringing the instrument to life, and the total self-acceptance he had gained from doing so. But not since he was fourteen had he experienced such perfect harmony. When he had learned about the Klinefelter's, he had come pretty close, and then again during Nina's first pregnancy, but for some odd reason, he fell just short.

Today he would try again.

He sits up, brushing the clarinet against his naked chest. The instrument feels cool. He keeps it there and pushes his wine glass further away and glimpses the exotic wood floor. When they had bought the house, the floor had been blonde. He replaced it with luxurious Australian Jarrah, which now feels hard underneath him.

He gets up from the floor and stretches his legs. He ambles over to the window, his clarinet in one hand. Though the rain has subsided, the air still looks misty. He jiggles the key in the security gate until he hears the lock snap. He opens the gate, liberated by the clanking of metal being released. Then he cracks open the window, knowing the sound will waft up and down the posh tree-lined street.

Yesterday, he would have tried to trap the music in his basement, although this has never been within a musician's gift. But sensitivity to his neighbours' inability to hear what he hears makes him try. Today, he doesn't care.

All he cares about is giving the clarinet life. Nowadays, they are both accustomed to a stage, so he stands in a streak of light. Geoff runs his finger over the mouthpiece once again and brings it up to his lips. He closes his eyes, trusting that the composition will come. He searches his mind like a computer searches files and comes up empty for what seems an inordinate amount of time. Finally, his mind releases a familiar tune: *Stranger on the Shore*.

He breathes deeply and blows into the reed. It vibrates against his bottom lip and releases a cacophonous sound. Though he feels panicky, he persists. He works his lungs harder than ever, trying to harmonize. At one point his chest feels like it's on fire and is going to implode, but he keeps blowing.

On that dismal, autumn day all those years ago, he had been impulsive. All he had wanted then was to hush his mother. This desperation had driven him to find the other side of dissonance through his instrument. Now all he wants to do is hush his inner voice, stop it from taunting him about the past, the present, and the uncertain future; stop it from calling him a misfit. And suddenly he discovers that to do this, he has to let it run wild, let this voice of his have its way with him. This is the only way he will become desperate; desperate enough to take charge again.

His eyes now clenched, he feels the reed against his lip. Its presence needles him when he allows the most dreadful, chaotic thoughts to come to mind: being fired from a top bank; struggling to get another job; and countless failing business ventures. He can hardly bear the thought of his wife finding out about his past homosexual experience, the world finding out about his cancer, his Klinefelter's, his inability to father his children. He feels himself trembling violently. He is a misfit, always has been and always will be. Because of this, he has never lived up to being a man. And worse yet, he is going to die prematurely. All he will leave behind is fucked-up truths.

Now he feels hot all over again. Still, he gives the clarinet all of him. Sleek and slender beneath his intense touch, the instrument appears to flirt with him. The sound it emits allures him. He knows there is no turning back now. He takes the music from the top. With every breath, he releases tension. The freer he feels, the more melodious the music sounds. He hangs onto the music for as long as his breath will allow.

When he feels himself pulsating, he knows it is time to let go. He must come clean with Nina. He must make amends with Peter and rescue the deal. He must give his children a decent inheritance; give them a chance of self-acceptance. He must put things right, all of it. Suddenly, the unmistakable sensation of harmony waves over him. In a slow flutter, it passes. Breathing heavily, he brings the music down and to a close. Slowly, he moves the instrument away from his lips, but he keeps hugging it.

At the sound of his wife's steady footsteps on the stairs, he comes out of the space. Now, he realizes he is drenched in sweat. Carefully and quickly, Geoff lays the clarinet on the windowsill and waits to face Nina.

Winter

*"If we had no winter,
the spring would not be
so pleasant: if we did
not sometimes taste of
adversity, prosperity would
not be so welcome."*

~Anne Bradstreet

The Seasons

THE MORNING AFTER THE INCIDENT, Sandy rose with the sun. His ninety-year-old wife Mary lay peacefully supine. Her coiffed silver hair looked as if she had just stepped out of the beauty parlour. Her chest moved faintly. He smiled and made his way to the bathroom. After dressing he ambled down the stairs and into the garage.

There, he stood and stared at his new BMW. She was not the Silver Wraith he had driven during the youth of his life, but still, she made him feel as vital. Then, he was a chauffeur for a member of the Royal family. But when World War II broke out, he lost his job and eventually ended up being a bus driver. That was one of the unhappiest periods in his eighty-four years of life, but thankfully it hadn't ended like his father's had. He too had been reduced from a chauffeur to a bus driver. Sadly, he had never quite come to terms with it, particularly after his accident involving a child. He had died aged fifty-eight, never again knowing the real pleasure of driving.

Sandy, on the other hand, took up driving as a pastime after retirement. He knew it gave him a lifeline. At first, he bought second-hand cars and traded them in every so often, but ten years earlier, he had bought his first new BMW. His most recent had arrived less than two months ago. His only daughter, Liz, thought he was an old fool, buying a new car. As far as she was concerned, he was too old to buy anything new. But he knew better. Life was about spirit rather than age. And he was spirited, if nothing else. That he had confirmed last night.

He went closer to the car and immediately noticed a fleck of green paint in the silvery grey door and then a long scratch along the body. He gasped and stepped back quickly, nearly tripping over his own feet. He turned away from the car and made his way to the back garden where he could appreciate the Sussex morning, and the beautiful spring-like atmosphere. It was forecast to be the hottest day of the year so far, and then cool down with showers. He decided to mow the lawn before the transition.

Afterwards, he admired the shimmering grass and then the matching rhododendrons he had planted last year. One had burst into colour. Although white, it was remarkable with pink speckles. The other was bare and sun-scorched. He sprayed it with water until its leaves flopped.

Mary came up behind him and cleared her throat. He turned around and noticed that she was looking at the sky. His eyes followed hers, fixing on the veil of pink hues above their heads. They both looked down and held each other's gaze. Her eyes, still like blue diamonds, had softened over the sixty-one years they had been married. But they continued to resemble those of the young woman he had wed: the girl with whom he had watched more sunrises and sunsets than he could remember. Her slender face had sunk, but in a lovely way that accentuated her eyes.

Mary burst into soft laughter. The wrinkles around her mouth danced. She kissed him on the forehead and told him she had laid out their morning tea. Not a word about last night. She had chosen to forget it. And though he would not speak of it again, he would never forget the horrible experience.

Driving in the luminous night on the way home from Yorkshire, where they had been for a week's holiday, he had relaxed in his thoughts. He didn't know what Liz was so worried about. At eighty-four, he was a great driver and even better at night. The moonlight sharpened his vision. Not only did driving keep him alive and well, but he also loved it, and wasn't prepared to stop yet, if ever, no matter what she said.

Now and again his eyes flitted to Mary. They had been through much of what life had to offer together, both ups or downs. They had loved and lost, including burying their parents, a child, and many friends. Yet they both carried on as if it life had much more to offer. Still, they loved driving to Yorkshire for short breaks now and again. His one surviving friend, who no longer had the will to do anything, reckoned that driving kept Sandy lively. He encouraged him to stick with it, no matter what. Sandy knew he was right.

Suddenly, another car nudged his bumper, forcing him out of his thoughts. Startled by the intense glare of the headlights overshadowing his car, he sped up and then noticed in his wing mirror a vehicle drawing up beside him. He slowed down. In seconds, a large jeep-like vehicle pulled up close. The driver honked. Sandy wondered if something was wrong. He touched the control, one of the many gadgets on the steering wheel and cracked his window. The passenger, a bearded man with a scrunched-up face, hung his head out of the car and motioned for him to pull over.

Sandy's heart hammered with fear. Before he could speed up again, the jeep came over into his lane, and bumped his BMW from the side, coercing it on to the verge. He gripped the steering wheel, keeping his car from swerving, but it did come to an abrupt stop when he hit the breaks. Mary stirred, raising her head. The man in the jeep was flinging his arm out of the window. Was he trying to reach into their car?

Sandy pressed button after button, turning on and off the windscreen wipers, the radio, until finally, the window shot up. The man jumped out of his car and banged on the window and pulled on the door.

"Who's that man?" Mary cried. "What's going on?"

Sandy could not respond to her. His heart revving, he somehow stamped on the accelerator and pulled the car back on the road. Before long, however, the jeep shot past him, honking the horn intensely. Still he kept speeding along, driving faster than he had in years.

"What are you doing?" Mary screeched. "Slow down! Let them go, you old fool! What are you doing? Liz was right! You shouldn't have bought this car. Slow down! Stop it!"

He drove with the precision of a much younger man. His flabby arms turned firm and his adrenalin flowed like a rushing river. Somehow he caught up to the jeep, overtook it and lost any sign of it. Shortly afterwards, he slowed down and felt himself trembling, so much so that he turned off at the next exit where he thought there was petrol and food. But it was derelict.

Nervously, he put the car into its parking gear and tried to quieten his breathing. Mary sat with her arms crossed, tears spilling down her face. He searched his mind for an explanation for his frivolous behaviour. He should have let the hooligan go ahead, but before he could say anything, the utility vehicle swung in from nowhere. It circled around them, and then backed up, stopped at a distance and barrelled towards their car. There was no time to think, to do anything. He felt Mary pulling at him and heard her screaming from a deep place within that she had not used in years.

"Do something!" she said. "Do something, you old fool!"

But he was frozen with fear, inadvertently waiting for death to hit. However, it passed them by like a gust, swishing and missing the car. The vibration reverberated in his head for minutes. Still in a daze, he peered in the rear-view mirror and saw the two young men, heads hanging out of either side, cackling.

Somewhere lost in their noise, he heard Mary's whimper. When he reached over and patted her hand, she winced. Still, she asked him if he was all right.

He nodded and put his trembling hand on the handle to open the door.

"What are you doing?" Mary asked.

"I'm going to look at the car," he said quietly. "Make sure she's all right."

"The car?" she said firmly. "What about us?" She looked around. "Those hooligans could come back at any time."

Sandy swallowed hard and took his hand off the door. He sat frozen.

"Let's go home, please!" she said sharply. "Please!"

Sandy put the car in gear, driving back to the road and all the way home. They had not spoken a word all the way there; not a single word. Even when they got home, not a word was said. But now on this beautiful morning, life between them was warm again.

After tea, he moved from one task to another: gardening; putting out the bird feed; cooking; working on the computer; and cleaning. He and Mary did not talk unnecessarily, but that was normal. What time would she like tea? Would she like him to record their favourite game show?

He kept moving about to feel his own blood flowing through his veins and to keep his mind off the incident. He felt the need to drive again, if only to prove to himself that he could do it. But he didn't dare mention the car for fear that Mary would be reminded of last night.

The next day, however, he woke with the intention to drive. But when he tried to rise, he found he could barely move. After wriggling and repositioning himself, he sat on the edge of the bed, his feet feeling as if he had stepped on shards of glass. At last the pain climbed through his legs to his back and there it sat. After ascertaining that he could not get up, they telephoned his doctor, who suggested ibuprofen.

Mary wanted to call Liz, who lived in the States, but Sandy rejected that notion. The last time Liz had come when he had a back problem, she had stayed for two weeks and shattered their nerves. She reminded them they were elderly and should therefore act like it.

She chastised him for having a car at all, let alone a new one. And she had hired a nurse and a cleaner and as soon as she left, he had fired them both. He could not tolerate her insolence.

After the ibuprofen miraculously kicked in, he got up and went straight to the garage. He reversed the car out of it, let the window down and felt heat rush in. He put the air-conditioning on full blast and put up his window. Who would ever have thought he'd own such a car? He had a mind to drive to the seaside, not that far away.

The best of the day was gone; it was late afternoon now. Soon the rain would come. He wanted to enjoy what was left of the sunshine. He tooted the horn for Mary. She came outside, looking disconcerted.

"What about a drive to the seaside?"

"You've lost your head!" she said.

He smiled at her mischievously.

"All right, then," she said. "Let me get my handbag and lock up the house."

When they got there, they sat in the car and watched the sea gulls launch themselves like they were airplanes. Some landed on water; others on the pavement. He rather enjoyed it, but after a while, Mary seemed bored.

He daydreamed of having one of those remote-controlled boats, watching it on the water and hearing the waves crash. He turned to tell Mary his idea and noticed her snoozing. Looking to the greying sky, he knew it was time to get back. Still he took the long way around, stretching his arms out before him and clutching the steering wheel firmly. It felt good to be driving. It really did.

Suddenly, Sandy heard a honking horn coming from behind. He looked up to see that he was holding up traffic, tootling at best. Thankfully, there were two lanes. Sandy pulled out without looking behind him and cut into the path of another car. The driver honked and overtook him, shaking a fist.

Now Sandy pulled over to the roadside and brought his car to a halt. He heard a thump. "What in the dickens was that?" he said aloud. His eyes darted over to Mary. She was still asleep. Wondering how she could sleep through all that, he shook her. But she didn't wake up. Focusing on his wife, he was shocked to feel the car tremble. A fat man, his stomach protruding from his T-shirt, whacked the bonnet with his fist. Taken aback, Sandy ensured the doors were locked. From the look of the man's fiery eyes, Sandy had somehow upset him. Though he shouted obscenities, Sandy could not make out what he was saying. Then the man lifted a yappy dog to the window.

Sandy thought of his father's tragic ending. While on a bus route one day in London, he had accidentally hit and killed a little girl. That same day, the girl's traumatized father told Sandy's father that the child had run into his path. There was nothing he could have done about it. Still he had never recovered from taking another's life.

Sandy swallowed hard. He looked at Mary and saw she was still unmoving. He reached out to touch her, but pulled his hand back suddenly. He rested his head on the steering wheel, feeling a hot sensation creep from his neck to his back. He felt paralyzed but somehow, he managed to put the car in gear. He had to get Mary home.

By the time he got there, he had experienced a lifetime of emotions. He thought of when they were young lovers, then becoming parents of twins and losing one of them before she was even one, and how this had strengthened their love for one another. He'd always believe that their overwhelming love for Liz helped her to be a strong independent girl. The doctors had said she'd never get over the loss of her sister, but she did. And when Mary had cancer and nearly died, they overcame that too. They never seemed to reach the end of the road, no matter how old they were. But now, he realized, they were there. He had no idea how he would cope with it. He felt cold and bereft.

In the driveway, he brought the car to a stop. He glanced at his wife, wondering how he was going to tell Liz. That would be the worst part...saying it. He knew he should call an ambulance, but he wanted to get his wife inside first.

Tears ran down his face as he got out of the car. Stiffly, he walked to the passenger side, opened the door and leaned over to undo her seat belt. The pain that shot up through his back was almost unbearable. As if Mary sensed him, her eyes popped open like a blooming flower. She pushed him off of her, reminding him that they were too old for hanky-panky. Sandy's knees buckled. He nearly toppled backwards but he caught himself, somehow landing on his bottom on the pavement.

Another wave of pain stabbed at his back, as he watched his wife fling her legs out of the car, both at the same time. She hovered over him, determined to help him up. She yanked at him. He patted her hand and squeezed it. She didn't understand. Suddenly, the pain overtook him and he eased back, reclining on the ground. The heat of the pavement bought some relief. With the heavens breathing down on him, chills travelled through his body. The sky had darkened in most places and the others were patches of varying grey.

"Call someone," he told her, turning his eyes on her.

"Get up, Sandy Ansley," she said.

"Sweetheart, I can't," he said. "Call 999."

"What do you mean, you can't?" she asked, her blue eyes blazing. "You were just driving like a bat out of hell; nearly scared me to death. Now get up, dear!"

Thankfully, her voice faded with the sounds of a car crunching the gravel of their driveway. Distracted, she looked up. "It's the police."

Sandy heard a car door slam and then hurried footsteps. A young man talked on a radio.

"Can't you just help him up?" Mary questioned. "He doesn't need an ambulance. He went backwards being silly, that's all."

"He looks like he needs an ambulance," the young man said and squatted beside Sandy. "Are you Mr Ansley?"

"Yes," Sandy said in a low-whisper, noticing the young man's unblemished skin and bright eyes.

"Are you all right, sir?"

Sandy smiled affirmatively, even though in pain. After this, the police officer explained why he had come. He asked Sandy if he recalled hitting a dog.

"That's not true," Mary said. "I was in the car with him the whole time. He's an excellent driver. You should have been there earlier when he sorted out those young hooligans."

Sandy attempted to shush her, but she talked over him. Meanwhile, the young police officer wiped blood off the lower bumper. "I'll have to give you a citation, sir," he said quietly, "and ask you to go the DVLA to have your licence updated, Mr Ansley, before you drive again."

"Who's going to drive us to the shops?" Mary asked.

Sandy closed his eyes and blocked out the voices. He had no idea what the officer said to his wife. When the paramedics came, they sat Sandy up in front of the car for longer than he cared to look at it. The BMW's grey paint glimmered. Sandy could see his own reflection. He couldn't ignore his droopy face. His eyelids were thicker than he remembered and each wrinkle was an imperfection.

When the paramedics lifted him from the ground, Mary held his hand. They took him into the house. Inside, they explained that he had a collapsed vertebra in his spine. He could be in the house for a while. They gave him a jab to ease the pain. Before he slipped into sleep, he told Mary to call Liz.

"I can take care of us, love," she said, her eyes sparkling. "I know how you feel about having others in the house. And don't worry about driving. I'll take a taxi to the shops until you're up again." Her small lips parted into a half-smile.

Sandy felt overwhelmed, looking at his elderly wife. She knew how to protect his pride and he appreciated it, but deep within, he knew that the season had changed, and she must, too. There was no place for stubbornness in life's final season.

"We don't want you with a bad back, too," he said. "Call our daughter. She'll take care of it all. Sell the car."

Mary eyed him suspiciously. "Who's going to drive us, then?"

Sandy didn't answer. Suddenly, he heard thunder rumble and then the sound of rain. In Mary's greying blue eyes, he imagined spring, summer and autumn passing quickly and winter settling in.

How About That

SINCE SIX O'CLOCK THIS MORNING, I've been on the back porch in my rocking chair, rocking. Even though my housecoat is starting to feel sticky against my ole skin, I'm still rocking. I want to undo the buttons, take in whatever cool is left of the morning, but all I can do is hold on to the arms of the chair and keep on rocking.

I rock to the chair's squeaking sound and look out over the sprawling yard, and though my misty eyes fix on the spray of blooming flowers and two squirrels darting around them, I keep on rocking.

In the background, I hear the telephone ringing, but still I keep rocking. It rings again and again, and I keep rocking. I'm rocking fast now, real fast, just watching the naturalness of the day.

When I hear the sounds of footsteps rushing through the house, I can't concentrate anymore. That's when I wonder what time it is. A lump forms in my throat when I realize that I've missed my praying time.

Lawd have mercy, I ain't missed my praying time in ten years. Lawd have mercy, what does this mean?

Soon my daughter-in-law is standing over me staring and fretting. When I look at her, I see clean into her green eyes, now gone as yellow as an uncooked egg. I quietly ask the time, all the while rocking.

Dee doesn't answer but asks, "How long have you been rocking?"

I turn my eyes back to the yard and keep right on rocking.

"You didn't hear the telephone."

I don't answer and keep on rocking, focusing on some flowers that look like violet ribbons fluttering in the light breeze.

"Momma," she says. "Momma!"

Automatically, I keep rocking. She grabs the chair, her hands covering mine, and stops it from rocking. I wriggle my hands away from hers. She sighs and lets the chair go and stares for what feels like forever. Finally, she walks off. I start rocking again, this time my hands in my lap, and before long, she is right back beside my chair, talking about getting us some water and maybe a bite to eat.

I lower my eyes. Then she drops down on her knees in front of me and grabs hold of my chair again and stops it from rocking.

"Momma, look at me," she says. "Look at me. We got to face this together."

"What?" I ask, still looking down. "What?"

"You know what," she says. "Junior is gone, Momma. Junior is gone."

I feel tears stream down my cheeks and taste their salt. My eldest son is gone. Lawd have mercy, he is gone. I fold my arms and throw my head back on the chair. I shut my eyes and weep. Finally, I ask the Lawd how come he let me outlive both of my chirrun.

"Ain't a mother s'pose to go first?" I say, hearing the bitterness in my own voice. When I don't get an answer, no sign or nothing, I open my eyes and see Dee bowed as in prayer, her head hanging.

"What time it happened?" I ask.

She lifts her head slowly and looks at me, her yellow eyes confused.

"Knowing the time is important," I say, remembering that when my youngest son, Jesse, died, it was 0806 hours. The Air Force plane went down at 0806 hours. And every day for ten years, I've been lowering my head in prayer at 0806 hours, washing dishes, looking at the news, whatever, except today.

Now Dee is resting on folded legs, still looking at me. I feel the urge to reach out and touch her hair, caress it like she my little girl, but she's somebody else's daughter, not mine. Both my chirrun are gone—both of them.

"What time?" I ask again firmly.

"Six minutes after eight o'clock." Dee holds my stare. "The angel came at 8:06."

I feel warmth in my face. All I can say is "How . . . about . . . that?" How about that!

In a quick twist of emotion, I wonder out loud why the Lawd didn't spare Junior.

"He couldn't live like that," Dee says, like she got to remind me that Junior had a tumor in his brain and had been sick for a long time.

"The Lawd could have spared one of 'em." I feel the bitterness rise up in my chest.

"He didn't," she says. "He didn't. Anyhow, who are we to question the Lord? You never have before—not when Jesse died nor when Dad died. Why now?"

I ain't got no answer for her. All I got is a heap of questions, which I let escape from my lips. "Why has God turned on me? Why would He treat an ole lady like this? Why would He put any mother through this kind of suffering? Why?"

Now I'm rocking again.

Dee gets up like she is as old as me, grunting and pulling up on the arms of my chair. She sits in my husband, Sol's, old chair right beside me. Me and him used to rock like there was no tomorrow. Now she looks out over the yard, too. She starts rocking, too. Suddenly, the silence between us feels thick. After a while, her voice slices through it.

"I know how you feel, Momma. I know how you feel."

My first instinct is to tell her she doesn't have any idea how I feel. How could she? Then I remember that Dee had two miscarriages a while ago and ain't never gave birth to this day. Now she done lost her husband, too. Slowly, I reach over and pat her hand. She sort of squeezes mine. Then we sit in silence for a further spell.

I remember when Junior was born—he came early, a plump baby who grew into a toddler fast. And, though he never crawled, he walked early, too. As a child, he was so smart that he finished school one year early and then went off to the Air Force and retired early. Suddenly, the thinking gets too much for me, so I ask her when's the funeral going to be.

She hunches her shoulders and tells me whenever I want it to be. I feel the tension spreading over me, so I shift my body.

"Junior liked to do everything early, didn't he?" I say. "He was always in a hurry, wasn't he?"

"I guess so," she says, and takes a deep breath. "Now that I think about it, he was the one who insisted we elope. And he was the one who wanted to start a family right away, too. And when that didn't work, he moved on to the next thing. He did like to move on."

"Mm hm," I say. "Look like we better take a page from his book. Help him move on."

"Why don't we bury him the day after tomorrow if Regina gets here," Dee says.

I smile at the thought of seeing Regina. She's like a daughter, too. She was Jesse's wife, but she married again now, with three chirrun.

Even though we've settled that, Dee and I both rocking now, both chairs just a-squeaking. I might as well tell her my plans to go on back to Georgia.

"No use in me staying here no more."

Dee stops her rocking and leans toward me. She scrunches her face and holds her midsection.

"This is your home," she says of the big ole house we live in.

T'ain't my home, not without Sol, Jesse, and Junior, I think. The boys bought us the house when they got good jobs in the military and then come home with wives. We all stayed together for a while.

Jesse was the first to go, then wasn't no use in Regina staying. Then Sol died, and Junior and Dee insisted I stay. But now Junior is gone, I ain't got no reason to stay.

"I ain't got nothing in this house," I say.

"You've got me," she says firmly. "You've got me, Momma."

"Well, it's your house," I say. "You and Junior the ones who finished paying for it and paid taxes on it." I cut my eyes at her, see her lip quivering. "If you don't want to stay here alone, then sell it and go on back to where your momma is, chile. You can be a principal anywhere."

Now Dee is rocking again. She takes a handful of her stringy hair and twirls it. She ain't washed it in God knows how long, so busy tending to Junior.

"Stay here with me, Momma," she says, looking out over the yard. "Stay here, won't you?"

"I can't do that," I say. "Nice of you to ask, but, naw, I can't."

"Why not?" she says. "You're the only momma I've got. You know my momma has been dead for years. Why would you just up and leave?"

I don't know what to say. I guess she's the only child I got, too, but I couldn't have had this white woman. Couldn't have.

"How are we going to live like mother and daughter?" I say. "I mean, what is it going to look like for a white woman and a little old black woman together?" I shoot her a glance. "Folks think us crazy."

"I don't care what they think," she says. "If you go to Georgia, I'm going, too."

I sit up as straight as I can, looking at her, just a-rocking. *How about that?* I thinks, remembering when she came to us. She was so different to the woman she is now. She stayed shut up in her room like we was going to bite her. When she found out that us was just folks, too, no matter the color of our skin, she wouldn't leave our side. And she's still here.

I'd always thought it would be Regina to cling. But here Dee is. . . . Come to think of it, it was always her, sitting with me when Jesse died, cause Regina too broke up herself, there when Sol passed. Now it is just the two of us.

I swats at her, trying to stop her from rocking. "No, siree," I say, rubbing my eyes. "I can't have folks bothering you in that hick town in Georgia where I come from. White and black folks still 'spicious of each other there."

"That was a long time ago," Dee says. "We will be just fine wherever we are. But if you're worried, we should just stay here. Shouldn't we?"

"I reckon so," I say, still, however, remembering them chirrun pouring syrup into her car's engine cause she married to a black man, right here in Maryland. "I reckon so."

Dee stops rocking and looks over at me for a long time. "That's settled then," she says, standing. She beckons for me to come out of the rocking chair. I lean forward. She helps me up. Though stiff, I feel surprisingly light. We walk down the steps, arm in arm, and then to the swing in the yard. There we have sat for many hours, more than I can remember, talking about any and everything.

Dee helps me unbutton my housecoat. The breeze flows in and cools me down. Then we sit and swing slowly.

"Don't worry, Momma," she says. "The world has changed."

I nod and think about what she says. I somehow know she must be right. She and I are sitting here like mother and daughter. How about that? And we got ourselves a black president. How about that? How about that!

We sit quietly, swinging. Listening to the swing hum softly, I feel the light wind against my chest and then my face, offering a whiff of fresh air. I take my daughter-in-law's clammy hand. She holds mine, too.

And clear out of the blue, she says, "How about that."

Acknowledgements

For support, inspiration, and constructive feedback, I am forever grateful to Jacob Ross and also Natasha Mostert, who willingly reads my original manuscripts. Other initial readers to whom I am thankful are Sarah Clark-Dixon, Karen Phillips, and especially Paul, who continuously provides all-around support.

For editing, I am grateful to both Jill Mason and Gale Winskill, and for a beautiful cover, I thank Karrie Ross. For PR, I am eternally grateful to have Helen Lewis on board.

Read more Sonja Lewis:

The Barrenness

The Blindsided Prophet

Now available from Prymus
Publications, London

The Barrenness: an excerpt

CHAPTER 1

Lil

Aunt Mamie's words are always hard to shake. Her words from their phone conversation the day before sit at the pit of Lil's stomach and haunt her. She cannot keep her mind on her work. All she seems capable of is staring out the window and remembering.

"Just remember what I said about time," her aunt said, as if Lil could forget.

Gripping the telephone to her ear, Lil watched the rain come down in sheets. She'd heard her aunt's opinion about having a child loud and clear. But women were having children later these days, weren't they? She had time as far as she was concerned. She wasn't quite forty yet. And she really didn't see what all this had to do with womanhood, not really.

"Lil, you still there," Aunt Mamie said.

"Yeah," she answered and changed the subject. "It's coming down pretty hard out there, isn't it?"

"At least you made it home in time," Aunt Mamie snapped.

In time for what, Lil wondered, having pushed the Porsche to top speed to cut the three-hour drive from Atlanta to two and half, but she didn't dare ask for fear that she'd be pulled into an unpleasant conversation about her aunt's day of reckoning, all she seemed to want to talk about these days—and, of course, Lil having a child.

"Listen, Aunt Mamie, I'm really sorry I didn't make it yesterday, but I couldn't miss the crisis meeting. You know that. Barbara would never let me hear the end of it."

"Is what your boss thinks all you care about? There's other things in life. Humph!"

Lil rolled her eyes, glad that her aunt couldn't see her. "Anyhow, speaking of other things, I brought you something pretty." Her aunt was eerily silent. "I won't say what it is, but I will say it's mauve. It's just a little something, but you'll love it, Aunt Mamie. You'll see tomorrow."

Mauve was her aunt's favorite color—surely she would be pleased. But she didn't even respond. Lil couldn't understand why Aunt Mamie was being so stubborn. She'd never been the easiest person to get through to, but normally, she came around. They had been like mother and daughter for nearly thirty years.

Lil's mother died when she was ten, leaving her and her two sisters with their father, a busy high school principal. In the beginning, Bud Lee would tie his necktie with one hand and scramble eggs with the other, simultaneously, like he didn't need help, though his childless sister lived next door. But after a few episodes of burned dinners, bleached-out clothing, and tangled hair, he must have concluded otherwise. Though the girls objected at first to this seemingly hard-hearted woman meddling in their business,

Aunt Mamie became their surrogate mother until their father remarried and moved them to Ohio. Lil was twelve then and had no interest whatsoever in moving.

She wanted to stay in Georgia. There, she would always be reminded of times when life was certain, as certain as her mother's presence. There, she didn't have to deal with cold weather and cold people, like she did in the poky town of Steubenville, Ohio.

But her father refused her pleas and moved her to the place with steep hills and harsh landscapes anyhow. He did, however, agree that she could visit Georgia in the summertime, so every summer she took a Greyhound bus a week after school turned out and endured the long, rambling journey with the help of a good book. She could count on Aunt Mamie to be at the Riverview Station waiting for her.

The older she got, the more she looked forward to the summer, in spite of Georgia's stagnating heat. The truth was, on the Buildings, she didn't have to worry about anybody making her uncomfortable—not anybody, not her peers and not her shady uncle-in-law, Mickey. She hadn't thought of him for years, but she would never forget him.

Anyhow, ten years ago, she had taken a job with Cosmed, making it possible for her and Jerome to move back to southwest Georgia permanently, to be near her aunt and her husband's family. At work, she had a quick rise to the top, but it didn't do her marriage any favors. Jerome strayed. So just over a year ago, she had finally kicked her husband out. Enough was enough.

Now Aunt Mamie lived in a nursing home, not quite the same as her small, cozy house on the Buildings, but God willing, she would return home soon, to pick up where she left off, and Lil would visit her there. Until then, Lil saw her at the nursing home every week. Yesterday had been her first miss in three months. Didn't history count for something?

When lightning flashed across the room, she knew her aunt would hang up soon, whether she had something to say or not. Aunt Mamie couldn't stand talking on the phone or doing anything that required electricity or water during bad weather.

"I'll see you tomorrow, Aunt Mamie. I might even knock off early."

"Humph, it'll be all over by then," her aunt said as the thunder roared.

"What will be all over?" Lil couldn't help asking.

"The storm," her aunt said. "Anyhow, just remember what I said about time." Her aunt hung up. Lil stewed, gazing out the window.

NOW LIL DROPS INTO HER CHAIR and starts working on the crisis strategy. She slips her feet in and out of her high heels. Her eyes feel dry, her eyelids heavy. She has tried every remedy she knows—ibuprofen, a macchiato, sparkling water—to get rid of the veil hanging over her eyes today, but it dangles there along with her thoughts of her aunt. She drops her pencil onto the desk.

When they last saw each other, her aunt had said something to Lil about her womanhood slipping away with time if she didn't have a child. And she was obviously making the same point again last night.

The phone buzzes, causing her to flinch.

"You have an urgent call on line one," her secretary says.

She grabs up the phone. "Aunt Mamie?"

"It's Will," her aunt's stepson says in his brittle, scraggly tone. She pushes the hold button and takes a deep breath.

"Jennifer! You didn't tell me it was Will Owens."

"You didn't give me a chance."

Will has never called her before. She does not trust him. She can't say why, except he has inserted himself into her aunt's life in a strange way. Lately every time she has visited the nursing home, he's been sitting at the foot of the bed, following her movements with his curious eyes. Thank God, her aunt shooed him off the last time she was there.

"Did he say what he wants?"

"No, but he said it's urgent. He's your aunt's son, right?"

"Stepson." She returns to the call and shudders at the sound of his heavy breathing. "Hi, Will, what can I do for you?"

He grunts, grating on her nerves. "Momma2 passed in the middle of the night."

Lil reaches for the stress ball near her computer. Her fingers encircle it and squeeze it. She can feel her chest constricting and the faint pressure of her aunt's pearl necklace around her neck. She can't have heard him right. She wants to ask him to repeat himself, but her voice is stuck in her throat.

"You act like you didn't hear me. I said Momma2 died last night."

This time her brain processes his words. Momma2 is Aunt Mamie; Aunt Mamie is Momma 2. She feels as if a rug has been pulled from underneath her, though she is sitting. It's similar to the way she felt when her mother died. Then her father had been there to hold her up, offer his shoulder to lean on and cling to. Now all she has is a plastic telephone with the harsh voice of a stranger delivering the news.

"This can't be right," she says, her head spinning. "I mean, I just talked to her last night."

"So did I," he says.

By now, the dizziness is so powerful that her head is pounding, as if something were chipping away at her temple. "I don't understand. She sounded well when I talked to her. What happened?"

"She died," he says. "A natural death in her sleep."

She feels the tiny hairs on the back of her neck stand up. She props the telephone on her shoulder and intensely rubs the back of her neck.

"I ain't surprised," he says. "She tried to prepare us."

As much as she hates to admit it, he's right. "I'll call Foster's straight away," she says.

"For what?" he asks. "I've already called Baine's. They're going to pick up her body later this morning."

"You'll just have to call them back." She nearly drops the phone as she continues to massage her neck, which feels like it is on fire. "The funeral home is Foster's. It's in her will."

"I ain't calling nobody back. The decision to go with Baines is final."

"You need to call them back, Will. Tell them." She raises her voice, feeling her body lift out of the chair at the same time.

"All I need to do is stay black and die."

"Who put you in charge?" she asks, ignoring his comment. "Why did the doctors call you, anyhow?"

Will stalls, but she knows the answer. The bastard probably told the doctors not to talk to anyone except him. He did that the last time her aunt got sick, but Lil's father had set him straight, told him to his face not to disrespect Lil ever again. After all, she was the closest thing her aunt had to a child. "Did you tell the doctors not to call me? Is that why they called you?"

"For the record, the doctors didn't call me," he says. "Papa called me. He is her husband, remember? Papa—her husband. He the one thought you would appreciate a phone call. But I see that was a mistake. Don't worry about me trying to do you any more favors."

"You do me a favor? Give me a break. I have just as much of a right to know as you do, if not more. I'm her closest relative here, or have you forgotten?"

"Papa is her closest relative anywhere, Lil Lee. Get a grip, girl."

Lil pulls the phone away from her ear again and curses under her breath. "I don't want to talk about this anymore. I will be there as soon as I can."

"For what?"

"You know for what!"

"No, I don't know. We ain't changing the funeral home if that's what you think. And everything else is going to get done with or without you."

Now Lil wants Will to stay out of the matter altogether. He's messed things up enough already. In fact, she wants him out of her aunt's life—out of her death, to be more specific. And that means getting him out of Aunt Mamie's house. He has been staying there since her aunt and his father moved to the nursing home. "You'll need to move out of Aunt Mamie's house as soon as possible."

"Why?" he says. "It's my house now."

"That is a lie!" She hears the firmness in her voice.

"Bullshit," he says. "Momma2 left the house to me."

"Aunt Mamie left her house to me. It's in her will. You must know that."

Will's sudden quietness gives her the feeling she has pushed him beyond anger. Then without any warning, his voice erupts in a heated flow. "No, I don't know that, but I tell you what I do know, bitch. She left the house to me, and I am not moving!" He slams down the phone.

The phone slides from its safe place between her shoulder and neck and falls to the floor. She doesn't bother to retrieve it, just sits trembling and clutching the pearls around her neck.

The Blindsided Prophet: an excerpt

CHAPTER   1

BEHiND THE WOODS

A person's color was more than color in the town of Coffee. It was either a curse or a blessing. For most folks with skin the color of sand, it was a blessing, but for Lydia Brown it was a curse—a curse because her skin was a different color from her daddy's. He was as black as dirt and she as light as sand. And because of this, everybody said he wasn't her daddy. The children at school taunted her all the time. But he was her daddy, doggone it, in every sense of the word. He protected her from their sharp words, and from boys trying to make her go further than she wanted to; he cooked for her every day—grits and eggs and fish before school, and after school he cooked fish again in more ways than most women knew how to do. And hush puppies. And he talked to her and listened to her. He was her daddy!

She always wondered how come her daddy didn't marry after her momma died, in the mid 50s. Lydia was only nine. He must have had girlfriends, but she never saw them, except Miss Henrietta, who used to sew for them, make him nice suits and her pretty dresses. But Miss Henrietta didn't act like a girlfriend, a wife to be. She didn't fuss over Ike Brown, cook for him, and warm his bed like her mother had. And the woman was scared of everything—a frog, a bug, like she hadn't lived in the country her whole life. Lucy Brown, on the other hand, would pick up most insects and put them back outside. She didn't seem afraid of anything, except maybe that old white lady on the other side of the woods.

One day about a year before her mother died, Lydia and her mom wandered farther than usual into the woods. They went across the creek and came out to another area where Lydia had never been. They took a winding path and came to an opening in the trees. From there, she could see a path, which led to a huge house.

"Wait for me here," her mother said, pointing to a massive oak tree. "I'll be back in a few minutes."

Lydia nodded, but as soon as her mom took off, she left the tree and followed at a distance. She'd done it many times before on the other side of the woods and watched as her mom killed a snake or something. This time when her mother came out to a huge yard that led to a plantation house, Lydia stayed at the edge of the woods behind another tree, fixated. She had never before been this close to one of the big houses she had seen from the roads or heard her friends talk about. Their moms cleaned at those places. She'd had no idea one was just across the woods.

Lydia could make out a figure sitting in a rocking chair on the porch, looking into the wide-open yard. As her mother moved closer to the porch, the figure stood. It was an aging white lady, her hair the color of oak moss. The girl hated the feeling that rose in her. She hugged the tree and watched. The lady rushed into the big plantation house and soon came back out with a rifle. She aimed it at Lydia's momma, who just kept on walking towards her. Lydia heard herself screaming, but her sound must have been lost with the firing of the rifle. Her mother stopped but didn't fall. As the shot rang out, Lydia's heart felt like it was going to come out of her chest.

She tore out and ran to her momma. Suddenly, the white lady, still gripping the rifle, fixed her gazed on them. Then a little boy, not as tall as her, with a crew cut, came running out of the house and clutched at the woman's legs. While trying to free herself from the boy, the lady somehow managed to set the gun off again. It blasted in the air. A stocky black lady ran out of the house then, and the white lady gave her the gun, yanked the crying boy by the hand, and stomped into the house. Lydia's momma caught hold of the hem of her long dress and fiddled with it.

"Where my momma and daddy," she asked.

"They ain't here no more," the black woman said. "Go on back where you came from now and don't come again."

"I got rights to come here, Hattie," she said. "This my home as much as it is yours."

Hattie looked over her shoulder, cradling the gun. She shot Lucy a heated stare. "It ain't safe for you to come here, Lucy Bell," she said. "Now go on, I say."

Suddenly, Lydia's mom took a step forward. But before she could take another one, Hattie stopped her, aiming the gun at her. Lucy then backed down, grabbed her child's hand and fled to the woods. Though her grip was painful, Lydia endured it and questioned her momma all the way to the creek. "What's the matter, Momma? Why did that lady have a gun? Why did the black lady say not to come there anymore? Why did she act like she was going to shoot you?"

Lucy Brown didn't answer until they reached the creek. "They making like Momma and Daddy stole from them," her mother said and nearly stepped into the water without gauging it, though she had told Lydia about the dangers of the waters many times. Aside from the turtles and eels that might snap at or entangle you, you could easily wade too deep and lose your balance. Sometimes Lucy would stoop and see how far she could reach down. If her arm went under, she would keep trying until she could touch the bottom.

Not today. This time Lydia yanked *her* back, tested the water, and found a shallow crossing where even the little boy at the plantation house could have passed. Still, she held her mother's hand, scared she might lose her balance to the rocks and weeds. On the way there, Lucy Brown, though petite, had hoisted her leggy daughter onto her back and carried her over. But now she trembled and looked disoriented. When they got to the other side, Lucy headed straight for the old hut instead of the new house that Ike had built with his own hands.

"Come over here," she told her daughter.

Lydia moved slowly towards her. Lucy stared so hard that Lydia felt heat sweep over her face.

"Stop asking your daddy where you come from," Lucy said in that broken English of hers. The girl hated the way her words sang sadness. "Everybody comes from somewhere. You came from me. Be proud of that."

"Yes, ma'am," Lydia mumbled and gazed at her.

"What counts with a daddy is what he does, not who he is. And no matter what, stay away from the other side of the woods, you hear me?"

The girl would never forget those words, nor would she forget how raw her mom's eyes seemed then. Her skin looked vulnerable, like it would burst if you touched it. About a year later, Lucy Bell Adams Brown did burst, so to speak, and shrivel up. Lydia and her daddy buried her mother in the cemetery up the hill from the church. And Lydia never put her arm beside her daddy's again to compare their skin. He'd never have to tense up and look away sadly. The older she got, the more she understood that who she was wasn't about her color as much as it was about her experience. But she was curious about who she was biologically. She didn't want to hurt her daddy, so she didn't tell him when she decided to go back to that plantation house where her grandparents once worked. She remembered what her mom had said—not to ever go there—but she felt old enough the summer she turned seventeen to handle any danger.

It wasn't hard to sneak over there, because that summer she was in the woods every day with her daddy's blessings. He helped her fix up the old hut, clearing away grass, hoeing, sweeping, washing, and wiping. He put in a cement floor for her and added new pine beams to support the frame. He nailed a piece of plywood over the door to keep the animals out, so she entered through a window. Some days she read and others she studied plants and protozoa, all in preparation for college. She had big plans to become a horticulturist, even though her daddy wanted her to be a teacher. She didn't want to be a teacher unless it was a horticulture teacher.

She knew a lot about the swamps. There was more to it than just hoeing and weeding. She knew how to stop some plants from taking over others. Her momma said some plants were like some people—greedy. They took over everything around them if they didn't have rules. Lydia had one rule for them: They could only have so many in their family. That didn't apply to the springing blueberries and roaming swamp grass, though. They grew any and everywhere and brought no harm to others, just joy.

The day she decided to make the journey, she felt so restless in the hut, the air so hot she could hardly breathe. She didn't worry about her daddy because he didn't even know she knew there were houses on the other side of the woods. She set out right after lunchtime. At the creek, she rolled up the legs of her trousers and took her sandals in her hands. That day the water was high, so she hopped from stone to stone until she was on the other side. Immediately, the world changed. The woods were more like a pruned forest, tall pine trees lined up as far as she could see. All kinds of colors jumped out at her, but they were not bold and splashy like the purples and yellows on the other side. They were like arranged flowers in a vase.

She hadn't remembered this from when she was a child. Anyhow, she asked herself, what kind of woods were these? Weren't woods supposed to ramble a bit? It was fine to interfere to keep peace and harmony in the woods. It was like raising children, insisting that they didn't trample on one another. But to make all the children wear the same uniform seemed wrong. For some reason, this broke her heart.

She put her sandals back on and headed up the lengthy path, which, if she remembered correctly, would bring her to the grounds of the plantation house. The walk seemed longer than she remembered, but after about ten minutes she came to a narrow road with big oak trees planted across from each other. She could see the house at the far end. She stopped and hid behind what might have been the same tree she hid behind until the rifle incident all those years ago. Now she realized she was tense with fear of being caught, her head swimming with dread. What was she worried about? She had come this far, and all she wanted was to find out what became of her maternal grandparents. Without that information, she might never know her true roots. Still, what if she came into contact with the woman who had accused them of theft? Would she remember Lydia? How could she? Lydia had been a child. Anyhow, Lydia didn't believe they'd been thieves. not as hardworking as her mother had described them. But even if they had been, she didn't care. They were her grandparents. Suddenly, she felt weakness in her knees, as if her own naïveté lodged there. Then it hit her. She was worried about her color. That was it.

Though she had not had any racial encounters, she knew many girls who had. They said it was because she could pass for white that folks didn't bother her. She thought it was because she lived in the woods and only went to town for school and for groceries on Saturday. Then she was with her dad. Otherwise, she didn't see white folks. She knew of the terrible business of the KKK and the race riots, some as close as Riverview, about twenty-four miles north. It was the 1960s, after all. But in Coffee, racial lines were so clearly drawn—in the schools, churches, swimming pools, movie theaters, for example—that she hardly ever saw white people. It was as if whites and blacks had a pact. Don't bother me, and I won't bother you. But she sensed the impatience of the black families around Coffee and couldn't blame them. They were tired of living in the worst houses, working for peanuts, and sending their children to run-down schools. Amen to that one. No child of hers would read books so tattered and washed out that sometimes they couldn't even read a whole paragraph. And sit in classrooms that a cloud of dust hung over all the time, no matter what her daddy said.

It wasn't that he didn't want civil rights. She could tell he did by the way he scrunched his face and swallowed hard when he heard of an injustice against his people. But he didn't like trouble. And he told her more times than she cared to hear that he didn't want her near white men. It could only mean trouble, reducing her to a white man's whore. The first time he said it, they were eating supper. He just slid the words in between mouthfuls, and when she didn't say anything, he coughed as if he was going to choke.

He cleared his throat. "What I mean, Lydia, is I want you to have a peaceful life. You got to marry a black man for this," he said. "That's why I'm sending you to Riverview to college."

"I'll have my pick, won't I," she said.

"Yes, ma'am," he said. "You will." He pushed his chair back from the table.

Lydia was lucky. She only knew one other girl who was going to college. Most girls would be staying at home, starting families and cleaning the plantation houses. But not her, thanks to her daddy. She planned to finish college and come back and take care of him and the land. Her husband could come, too.

Still behind the tree, Lydia stilled her nerves, took the rubber band off her hair, and let it drop to her back, just in case she ran into trouble. She let the hypocrisy slide down her throat. She had to do what she had to do. No matter what anyone said, she knew she was black in every sense of the word. Her mother was black and of black parents—at least, one of them was black, had to be. The voices of southern white males drifted through the air now. She couldn't make out what they were saying, but it had to do with the woods, leveling the woods, the other side of the woods. Their thick drawls were followed by lighthearted laughter. As they neared the tree, her heart rate increased, it seemed, with every step they took. She squatted, hoping not to be spotted but peeping out to see them as they passed.

One of them stood real tall, as tall as her daddy, and the other was average height. They wore fedora hats and dark suits made of fabric thicker than her daddy's

Sunday suits that Miss Henrietta sewed for him out of the most expensive fabrics that she could get her hands on. Suddenly, the men stopped as if they had spotted something. She ducked and stayed as quiet as she could. Finally, their voices sounded again.

"He ain't got no rights," one of them said. "He's a nigger."

She craned her neck to see them. They were standing face to face, the shorter one looking up at the tall one, with one hand resting on his friend's shoulder. In the other, he held a cigar.

"You tell him that." The tall man let his voice drop to a deeper tone.

"I'll be glad to."

"Anyhow, did Kay tell you that he made a deal with Marshall almost twenty years ago that will be good for a lifetime?"

"Whose lifetime? Marshall is dead now—God rest his soul—and unless he got the deed to the land, it ain't foolproof. Those woods don't belong to nobody except God, now that Marshall's gone."

The tall man looked into the air. Then he looked down at his friend. "We don't need to start raising sand with coloreds now, or we'll have the whole posse from Atlanta all over Coffee, and no one wants that."

"I ain't worried about that. I want to do what my sister asked, and she said to run that man away from here, whatever I did. But I got to respect your feelings. You just lost your wife. I loved Kay too, but I still got my wife. So I'm gonna back off until you're more comfortable talking about this."

The tall man freed himself of his friend's hand on his shoulder and walked ahead. The shorter one stared at him for a few seconds, his cigar between his lips, and then he followed. Lydia waited until they were on the porch. They lingered there for longer than she wanted them to, both taking off their hats and looking out over the land. She moved back further behind the tree, and held her breath; when she thought they were inside, she shot back towards the woods. In her haste to get out of there, she slammed into a white boy, knocking him to the ground.

She tried to keep going, but he caught her leg, tripping her to the ground, too.